The moment they crossed the threshold, Preston took Lee Ann into his arms. He caressed her cheek with his fingertips, trailing down the curve of her neck, sending shivers of delight racing through her body.

She sighed with pleasure, and the sweet sound of it deepened Preston's arousal. Lee Ann wrapped her arms around his neck as the desire to give herself totally to him pounded in her veins.

"Let's go upstairs," he breathed in her ear.

"Lead the way," she whispered seductively.

He kissed her once more, twirling his tongue against hers, before they mounted the stairs together. When they reached the top, he opened his bedroom door and swept her up into his arms. He crossed the room and eased them both down onto the bed.

"I dreamed about this last night," she said softly.

"Now we can make it real," he said, before taking her lips with his own in a long, searing kiss.

Books by Donna Hill

Kimani Romance

Love Becomes Her
If I Were Your Woman
After Dark
Sex and Lies
Seduction and Lies
Temptation and Lies
Longing and Lies
Private Lessons
Spend My Life with You

DONNA HILL

began writing novels in 1990. Since then, she has had more than forty titles published, including full-length novels and novellas. Two of her novels and one novella were adapted for television. Donna has won numerous awards for her body of work. The editor of five novels, two of which were nominated for awards, she moves easily from romance to erotica, horror, comedy and women's fiction. Donna was the first recipient of the *RT Book Reviews* Trailblazer Award and currently teaches writing at the Frederick Douglass Creative Arts Center.

Donna lives in Brooklyn with her family. Visit her website at www.donnahill.com.

Spend
My Life with
You

DONNA
HILL

KIMANI™
ROMANCE

 KIMANI PRESS™

ISBN-13: 978-0-373-86196-5

SPEND MY LIFE WITH YOU

Recycling programs
for this product may
not exist in your area.

www.kimanipress.com

Printed in U.S.A.

Dear Reader,

Welcome to the exciting world of my brand-new family miniseries, the Lawsons of Louisiana. Following the success—thanks to you—of my Pause for Men and The Ladies Cartel miniseries, I began to think about what direction my next work would take. I'd been asked and had thought about doing a family series for a while and finally the opportunity presented itself. The idea of bringing to the page a dynamic, powerful, sexy, politically connected family began to take shape. And what better time than now to showcase the beauty and power of a black political family?

The first character that came to me full-blown was Rafe Lawson. OMG! I had a thing for him before he was even fully formed. Then there are his twin sisters, Dominique and Desiree—identical in looks but as different as apples and oranges. Justin is the youngest, dashing brother who you will see come into his own over the course of the series.

To kick things off is the eldest sister, Lee Ann. When she meets Jr. Senator Preston Graham, there's no telling what will happen between them, save for a little bit of scandal and a whole lot of passion.

I'm so excited about the Lawsons and I hope you will enjoy each and every one of their stories, beginning with *Spend My Life with You.*

I'd love to hear from you. Send your thoughts to dhassistant@gmail.com and be sure to tell a friend!

Until next time,

Donna

Chapter 1

Lee Ann Lawson leaned toward her dressing table mirror and fastened the diamond studs into her ears, just as the booming voice of her father called out to her from the other side of the Louisiana mansion.

"Coming!" she called back, tightening the belt of her white silk robe around her slim waist and wondering as she padded barefoot along the winding hallway what it was that he couldn't find. She smiled inwardly and prepared herself to fuss over her daddy for the next few minutes. She was stopped halfway when one of her twin sisters, Dominique, leaped out from her bedroom door, hands planted boldly on her round hips.

"Sis, would you please tell my darling dull twin that this dress does not show too much cleavage!" She flashed a scowling look at her mirror image, who sat demurely on a cushioned foot stool.

Lee Ann looked Dominique up and down. Of the

two, Dominique was always the flamboyant one, ready at the drop of a hat to be the center of attention. And her dress definitely did that. Cut in the front to nearly her navel, the sparkling silver floor-length gown barely held her size Cs in place.

"You sure your dolls aren't going to pop out and introduce themselves at the party?" Lee Ann asked, only half in jest.

Desiree covered her mouth and laughed. "Told you, Dom. And it's the same thing Mama would have said."

Dominique pouted. "I have a cover-up."

"Be sure you have it with you," she warned. She peeked around Dominique. "You look beautiful, Desi. And you, too, Dom," she said with a big-sister wink.

"Lee Ann!" Branford bellowed.

The sisters exchanged a knowing look as Lee Ann hurried down the hallway. The voices of her brothers Rafe and Justin floated to her from the main room below. She couldn't wait to see her handsome brothers all decked out. She tapped on her father's door.

"Come in."

She pushed the partially opened door and stepped inside. Even after five years, she still had not adjusted to the reality that every night her father slept alone and that their beloved mother was no longer with them. As the oldest girl, she'd stepped into the role of caregiver for her mother during her mother's long illness and then the caregiver for her family—her father in particular.

"Hey, Daddy. Sorry, I got waylaid by those girls." She laughed lightly and crossed the circular room to where her father sat on the edge of the king-size bed struggling with his cuff links. "Here, let me." Her slender honey-toned fingers moved expertly to insert the onyx cufflinks and fasten them.

"You fix me up just like your mama, God rest her soul," he murmured and affectionately patted Lee Ann's hand.

The ache in his voice twisted inside of Lee Ann and settled where it always did—in the center of her heart. She leaned over and kissed her father's cheek then sat back and adjusted his tie, turning her head right then left as she did.

Her father was one of the most powerful men in the state of Louisiana. Senior Senator Branford Lawson not only carried clout but respect across both sides of the aisle. Some of his closest friends were those who for the average person were only seen on television and in newspapers, but to her they were Aunt Hillary or Uncle Bill. At any given time, the Lawson mansion would become the epicenter for political gatherings. She remembered one day as a young girl waking up and seeing former president Carter sitting in the kitchen sipping coffee with her father.

It had been her mother, Louisa, who'd overseen the Lawson household and clan like the queen of England oversaw her country. She was the consummate Southern hostess, the nurturing but watchful mother and loyal and devoted friend. Lee Ann became the woman she was because of her mother.

Lee Ann pushed back the memories as they threatened to overtake her. With her mother's passing, Lee Ann stepped into her mother's role. It was a big responsibility, but she did it with love.

"Perfect," she announced of her handiwork. "Now stand up and let me take a good look."

Her father dutifully did as he was asked.

"Looking good, Daddy."

He leaned down and kissed her forehead. "That's what all the ladies say," he teased. Then he looked at her as if seeing her for the first time. He frowned. "Why aren't you dressed?"

Her right brow elevated. "That's what I was doing when I was summoned."

He pretended to miss her point. "Well, don't stand around," he said, flinging his hand in her direction to shoo her out. "Get yourself together. You know how I hate being late."

Lee Ann shook her head and grinned. "Yes, Daddy." She returned to her room, took her dress from the walk-in cedar closet and was wiggling into it when her brother Rafe came knocking.

"Now look at you," he hummed in that tone he reserved for when he wanted something.

Rafe leaned against the frame of her door, a glass of bourbon in one hand and his other hand tucked into the pocket of his tuxedo slacks, as smooth and sleek as a panther and just as deadly to the ladies. Raford James Lawson, the eldest of the Lawson clan, was a notorious playboy not only in the United States but abroad as well, although he swore, with a wink and a smile, that those rumors weren't true. At thirty-six, he was unattached, wealthy, handsome, smart and came from a powerhouse family. He'd been profiled countless times in major magazines as one of the country's most eligible bachelors, sexiest man and heir apparent to his father's Senate seat. Rafe would agree to the first two, but the last stood as a bone of contention between father and son. He'd rather spend his days traveling, loving women and playing his sax. Politics weren't in his blood. But his father wouldn't hear of it.

Lee Ann pursed her cherry-tinted lips and ran her hazel eyes along the long lines of her big brother. "A little early for bourbon, don't you think?"

"Never too early for bourbon, cher," he teased, raising his glass to her in salute before taking a sip.

"At least make yourself useful. Come zip me." She turned her back to him and waited for his real reason for descending upon her.

"Listen, sis…"

Here it comes, she thought. "Yes, sugah, what is it?" She turned around to face him, looked up into his bottomless black eyes, framed by silky lashes, and knew without question what women saw in her brother. And no matter how much warning they were given they kept coming.

"About tonight…"

"Yes?" She buttoned the top button of his shirt then began fashioning his bow tie.

"I know Daddy wants to show me around like some prized pony and have me glad handing all night, but there's this new blues club down in the Quarter. If I can get there before midnight, I can get in on the last set."

His smooth face and midnight eyes literally danced with excitement and matched the almost childlike urgency of his voice.

"Rafe," she cautioned. "You know how Daddy feels about that."

"I know, baby sis. That's why I need your help…to distract him while I get out of there," he cajoled. He leaned down to her ear. "Please."

Lee Ann playfully pushed him away. "Don't start your foolishness with me, Rafe Lawson. I'm not one of your starry-eyed ladies."

He chuckled. "You wound me, cher."

She put her hands on her hips and then wagged a warning finger at him. "I'll do this for you…again. But I'm warning you, Raford. You get yourself in any trouble tonight and you're on your own. Understood?"

"Yes, ma'am." He leaned down and put a sloppy wet kiss on her cheek.

"Aggg. You know I hate when you do that! Ruining my makeup. Get on out of here."

Raford laughed on his way to the door. "Love you, too," he called out.

Lee Ann shook her head in affectionate amusement, walked over to her dressing table mirror to inspect the damage then touched up her makeup.

"Lee Ann."

She turned. Her younger brother Justin had his head sticking in her door, the spitting image of their mother with his sandy-brown complexion, tight curly hair and to-die-for dimples. Although he was still growing into his looks, Justin was one handsome young man.

"Daddy said if you aren't down in two minutes we're leaving without you. I'm to make sure you get downstairs," he said with a twinkle in his eyes. They both knew that Branford Lawson was more bark than bite, and the last person he'd get on the wrong side of was Lee Ann.

"Coming. Don't you look handsome?" She crossed the room and stood in front of him. Lee Ann was the only one who could make Justin blush. He, like his brother, towered over their petite sisters, and Justin, at twenty-three, beat his brother out by an inch of Rafe's six-foot-three-inch height. By habit, she straightened his tie and smoothed her hands over his broad shoulders. "Let me get my purse and I'm ready."

The family filed into the waiting limo, and it sped off into the balmy Louisiana night.

By the time they arrived at the estate of Congressman Jeremiah Davis, the reception portion of the evening was getting underway. Waiters glided between the bejeweled guests with platters of mouthwatering appetizers and flutes of champagne. The thousand-dollar-per-plate affair was a fundraising event for the incumbent congressman. And with the downward spiral of the economy on the watch of the Democrats, he needed all the support he could get.

Jeremiah and Branford had been friends since they were in knee-highs and had followed each other throughout their school years, served as each other's best man at their weddings and were godfathers to their children. There was a bond between them that was stronger than most brothers, and the Lawson clan adored their Uncle Jerry.

"It's about time you all got yourselves here," Jeremiah said, kissing cheeks and shaking hands.

Jeremiah could only be described as round. Everything about him was round, from the top of his head down to his bowlegs. He often reminded Lee Ann of one of those children's toys that rocked back and forth and rolled around without ever falling over.

"Hi, Uncle Jerry," Lee Ann said, becoming enveloped in his hearty embrace. He held her back at arm's length and looked her over.

"Looking more like your beautiful mama with every passing day," he said softly.

Lee Ann smiled. What could she say? She'd run out of words from the often heard comment. A part of her felt so complimented to be compared to her mother, then there was another part that felt overwhelmed by the comparison that she felt she could never live up to.

Her sisters and brothers had already dispersed into the crowd. They'd been trained well, since they were old enough to be introduced to the world. They knew how to work a crowd, gain information without giving any, befriend newcomers and leave an indelible impression on everyone that they met. They were the epitome of the political elite family, which was often as much of a burden as it was a badge of honor.

Lee Ann slipped her arm through Jeremiah's. "And where is Aunt Lynn? I don't see her."

"Probably worrying the waiters to death." He chuckled good-naturedly. "You know your aunt. Walk with me outside. I need some air already."

Lee Ann laughed lightly, and it stopped as if a cork had slid down her throat. A warm wave fluttered in her stomach as they drew closer to the group assembled near the balcony.

She'd only seen him from a distance in the past, although she'd watched him closely during his run for the junior Senate seat and listened to her father extol his virtues. Although Lee Ann worked closely with her father as his personal consultant, she tended to steer clear of the interactions of the power brokers, rarely visited Washington and worked out of the family home or occasionally at her father's local office in Baton Rouge.

"Congressman," one of the ladies announced. All eyes turned in their direction.

Jeremiah let out a hearty laugh. "Now that's the way I like to make an entrance, introduced by a beautiful woman." The group dutifully chuckled. He turned to Lee Ann. "I'm sure most of you know Lee Ann Lawson, the real power behind the senator."

Lee Ann's face heated. She looked from one to the other. "He gives me too much credit."

"All deserved, my dear." He slipped her arm out from his and patted her hand. "Senator Preston Graham, have you met Lee Ann?"

"I'm sure if I did I would have remembered," he responded, his dark eyes doing a slow stroll across her face. He extended his hand toward her.

Lee Ann stretched out her hand, and he leaned down and kissed the top of it. "My pleasure." A smile teased the corners of his mouth. "I feel as if I already know you."

She tilted her head slightly to the side. "Why is that?"

"Your father talks about you all the time."

Her gaze darted away for an instant. "He does the same about you."

"Is that right? Hope it's all good." Light danced in his eyes.

"Yes, it is. He thinks very highly of you. And congratulations, by the way, on your win."

"I'm still getting my feet wet. Your father is an excellent mentor."

"That he is."

"Can I get you a drink?"

"Yes. Thank you."

After they both realized that he was still holding her hand, Preston chuckled. "Maybe it's a sign that we should go out together."

Lee Ann's soft laugh brushed against him like a caress. He tucked her hand in the curve of his arm.

"I'm surprised we haven't officially met before," Preston said as they crossed the expansive room.

"I try to stay behind the scenes except when my father needs me front and center." She smiled and tried to keep her feet moving one in front of the other even as the electric energy of Preston Graham bounced off her, short-circuiting her brain.

"You do a very good job of it, considering that you are his political adviser of sorts. At least that's my understanding."

"I do oversee his activities, but it's more like a personal assistant," she said.

They reached the bar. "What will you have?"

"A white wine spritzer."

He gave the order to the bartender and ordered a bourbon for himself.

"My brother's favorite drink," she commented as they were served.

"A man after my own heart," he joked. "And apparently the ladies, as well," he added with a lift of his chin in the direction of her brother.

Rafe was in a close conversation across the room with a stunning woman who Lee Ann hadn't recalled seeing before.

She shook her head in amusement. "Rafe does keep busy."

"And what about you? When you're not personally assisting your father, what do you do?"

She was thoughtful for a moment. "Running the house and keeping an eye on my sisters and brothers is pretty much a full-time job."

"It doesn't sound as if you allow time for yourself." He stared into her eyes over the rim of his tumbler.

Her heart fluttered. "I find ways to enjoy myself," she said in her defense.

Preston studied her for a moment and decided to let the topic go. "What's it like growing up with a father like Branford?"

They walked together to an available table and sat down.

Lee Ann's smile was wistful. "Where can I begin?" She gazed around the room. "My life has been pretty much like this for as long as I can remember," she said with a sweep of her hand. "Politics and parties and entertaining and being in the spotlight has been a way of life."

He heard something in her voice, a note of hesitancy, regret. He couldn't be sure.

"I would think it was pretty exciting." He sipped his drink and watched the muted light play across her finely etched features.

Her warm hazel eyes flickered across his face. "I suppose it would be looking in from the outside. But to us, all of the people who everyone else reads about were like family." She drew in a breath, reached for her glass and realized that her hand was shaking. She concentrated on bringing the glass to her lips without spilling her drink. "What about you?" she asked, steering the conversation away from herself, a topic that she didn't relish discussing.

Preston set his glass down, tilted his head slightly to the side, his full lips pressed lightly together and puckered out. "Well, I'm a product of a single teenage mom. Public schooling. My mama worked two jobs that added up to one most of my life." His dark eyes drifted away from Lee Ann. "She would tell me every day that she expected me to make something of myself. She wasn't working so I could grow up to be a nobody." The corner of his mouth jerked as the images of those days of "have not" flashed through his head. "As soon as I was old enough, I got a part-time job after school, packing groceries, delivering whatever needed to be delivered, flipping burgers, waiting tables. You name it, I did it at one point or the other."

"It must have been hard."

He looked directly at her. "I suppose to someone looking in from the outside," he said, playing with her statement to him. "But like you, it was the only life I knew. Sometimes I would see the other kids in their new sneakers or tooling around town in their daddy's car, walking into fancy houses." His face and voice took on a hard edge like a tide that suddenly rushed to shore pulling the sand out from under your feet—unexpected and scary. "I knew there was more out there than what was in front of me, and I had to find a way to get it. My life and my mama's struggling made me what I am. Determined and focused to get what I wanted. And I did, but I'm not finished yet."

Lee Ann held her breath anticipating what she wasn't sure. And then he smiled and the tide slowly receded, and she was standing on solid ground again.

"Don't mind me, I can get a little caught up in my own rhetoric sometimes," he said, catching the look of apprehension in her eyes. "Come dance with me." He stood and extended his hand, once again the dashing, gallant gentleman.

Lee Ann placed her hand in his, and he helped her to her feet. They moved onto the dance floor, and then she was in his embrace. And he was all around her, his arms, the lines of his body, his scent. Her head barely reached his shoulders, so she found herself resting it against his broad chest as they moved in harmony, swaying easy to the music of the band, and she had the oddest sensation that she had done this all before, with this man. It was all so familiar and right. But of course that couldn't be true. She'd never met him before.

Preston didn't want to give in to the urgent need to pull her closer, to feel her fully against him. The sensation of her being so close and still so far was messing with his head. The fresh scent of her hair, the barely there fragrance that she wore combined with the heat of her body had him coiled tight as a rattlesnake. He had to concentrate on the music, the aroma of food, the smatterings of conversation that floated around him to keep his mind off what she was doing to his body.

In as much as he wanted her closer, there would be no doubt about her effect on him if he did. She'd be sure to think that he was some randy fool who couldn't control his urges. He was almost thankful when the music ended. He needed some air and some space.

He released his hold around her waist and stepped back. She tilted her head up to look at him; the dewy softness of her lips, the light dancing in her eyes and the tiny pulse beating in her throat had him wanting to forget what was proper and simply take her mouth and sample it until they couldn't take it anymore.

"Thank you for the dance," he managed to say, his voice thick and jagged. "I'm going to go mingle a little."

"Oh…of course." She put on a practiced smile and wondered what she'd done wrong.

He took her elbow and walked her back to the table. "Thanks again for the dance and the conversation."

She offered a tight smile while she watched him walk away, and for reasons that she couldn't explain she felt like bursting into tears.

"Hey, baby doll, come on and dance with your big brother." Rafe curved his arm around her waist before turning her petite body into his.

His arms were strong, familiar and secure, and for a few minutes she could forget how small and insignificant she felt, which of course was ridiculous. It was just a conversation, a drink and a dance. No big deal.

"You're stiff as a board." He peered down at her. "What's wrong? Did he say something out of the way to you?"

She heard the sudden rise in his tone. The smooth

easy cadence was gone. Lee Ann dared to look up at his piercing dark eyes.

"Don't be silly," she soothed. "I'm fine, and no, he didn't say anything out of hand."

Rafe took a hard look over his shoulder, seeking out the young senator as if seeing him would somehow validate what his sister said. He turned back to Lee Ann. "You sure, because I have no problem sharing a few words with him man-to-man."

Lee Ann gently pressed her hands against Rafe's hard chest. "I can take care of myself. Thank you very much," she added with a slight smile.

He leaned down and kissed her forehead then skillfully moved with her around the floor. "All you have to do is say the word," he said, his protective instincts kicking into high gear. He'd always been that way with his sisters, since they were all little. He took great pride in being the big brother, and yes, it was true that he loved women but none more than his sisters and of course his mother. Lee Ann was the one most like their mother, and he was sure that was one of the reasons they were so close, as children and as adults. "I'll hang around if you need me to," he said.

"No, please. I know your lips are itching to play, so whenever you're ready just go on. It'll be fine. I'll tell Daddy something or nothing." She grinned at him.

The dance came to an end, and they walked across the grand ballroom out to the balcony. The air was still heavy and filled with the scent of a hot spring night. Beyond the cove of streets, the lights of the city peeped in and out, and the soft sound of the Mississippi rolled gently in the distance.

For a fleeting moment, caught in the beauty of the evening, Lee Ann wished that she was peering out into the night, whispering soft words and sharing light laughter with her own someone special.

"Looks like everyone who's anyone is here tonight," Rafe commented, taking a brief look over his shoulder into the main room.

"Well, you know Uncle Jerry never does anything halfway." She continued to stare out into the night.

Briefly Rafe put his hand around her shoulder, and she tilted her head to rest it against him. "Can I get you a drink, a plate of food?"

"Another spritzer would be nice, thanks."

"Be right back."

She inhaled deeply and reentered the ballroom, watched the milieu move around her and felt so apart from the activities. It was so unlike her she thought, not to be like a butterfly flitting from one guest to the next, enjoining and cajoling as if she was the hostess. Smiling, as was her habit as she passed familiar faces, she found herself back on the balcony, sure that her brother would instinctively find her.

She leaned against the balustrade with her back to the Mississippi, and her stomach quivered when she saw Preston heading with purpose in her direction. She tried to glance away, ignore his approach, but it was too late.

He walked right up to her, cutting off everything and everyone around them. He took up her vision.

"I'm usually much more the Southern gentleman than I was earlier," he said. Thick lashes lowered over his dark eyes for an instant then settled on his face. A half-shy smile tickled the corners of his rich mouth. "I… You rattled me, Ms. Lawson," he said. The soft twangy cadence of his voice was both charming and unnerving.

Lee Ann tilted her head slightly to the right, for the first time since they met having a sense of standing on firm ground without her legs wobbling beneath her. She smiled and, always the tactful lady being Louisa Lawson's daughter, said, "Senator Graham, I have no idea what you mean."

The imaginary rift they'd created was crossed with their relieved laughter.

Chapter 2

"Where's that brother of yours?" Branford asked as the family headed out to the waiting limo.

The siblings shared a look behind their father's expansive back.

"If you think I don't know that he snuck out of here to go into N'awlins to play that damned sax of his at some juke joint, think again."

"Don't think they call them juke joints anymore, Daddy," Dominique said. Mischief sparkled in her eyes and tickled the corner of her mouth.

The quartet stifled their giggles. Dominique was notorious for intentionally pushing their father's buttons. He threw her a thunderous look over his shoulder, and she looked back at him in wide-eyed innocence. Branford simply shook his head and muttered to himself about "damned children."

* * *

They all tumbled into the limo still sailing on the high of the evening, still amazed that no matter how many of "these things" they attended they always had a good time. Dominique, Desiree and Justin were totally immersed in conversation. Lee Ann, who was seated near the window, took the opportunity to steal a few moments for herself, retreating to that space in her mind and spirit where she was carefree, devoid of responsibility and worry about anyone other than herself. She rested her chin on her palm and glanced out at the rolling panorama that sped in front of her: the stately homes that once served as plantations, the lush greenery, manicured lawns and the distant sound of ships sailing along the river to parts unknown to her—adventures maybe.

She drew in a long breath of calm, and the subtle scent of Preston wafted beneath her nostrils, triggering a surge of sensory delights. The feel of the pressure of his hand on her waist, the beat of his heart when he held her close against him while they danced, the way his voice vibrated through her when he leaned down to whisper something outrageous about one of the guests. For her, the evening had turned from ordinary to something special.

She wanted to see him again, she realized as the evening progressed then began to draw to a close—away from work and politics and parties. And it was as though he mimicked her thoughts, and he said the very words that were playing in her head. Still, as much as she'd wanted him to ask, had almost willed it, his asking surprised her. At first she thought he was asking just to be nice, to make up for that awkward beat that had happened between them earlier in the evening or like most eligible men in Louisiana who wanted to get close to her father through her.

"Before you start thinking anything beyond what I asked you, I want us to be clear about one thing."

Her brow arched in question.

"I'm my own man. Everything I have I worked for, I earned. So don't you think for a hot Louisiana minute that my wanting to see you is because of your family name and your daddy." He grinned. "I have both. That no good SOB who fathered me is out there somewhere," he added.

Lee Ann tossed her head back and laughed from the bottom of her feet. Her delighted expression stirred Preston in a way that he couldn't put into words, and all he needed was for her to say yes, give him something to look forward to, and she did.

"You're mighty quiet over there, sis," Justin said, drawing her back from her momentary retreat. "Everything okay?"

Lee Ann patted his arm. "I'm fine. Just a little more tired than I thought."

Desiree yawned. "Me, too. I can't wait to lay my head down."

"I could go for a few more hours," Dominique said. "Wish I would have snuck out with Rafe. Bet he's having a ball."

Lee Ann chuckled to herself and heard her father's snort of disapproval even as he pretended to be sleeping. This was her family, she thought with loving amusement.

* * *

Preston was thankful that the reception the prior evening was on a Friday night and not one of the typical midweek galas that zapped you for the rest of the week. He never did understand why so many fundraisers and political dinners were invariably on Tuesday. He laughed to himself as he continued on his early morning jog. Jogging was the one thing he tried to do on a daily basis no matter what his life was like the night before.

Running through his neighborhood, around the park and along the familiar pathways always invigorated him, cleared his head and stimulated his blood. Whenever he had a complicated issue to tackle with his constituents or had to break down the complexities of a bill that he needed to vote on, running always helped. When he was a kid and he saw the often defeated look on his mother's face, he ran to keep from crying and to run from the world that had him grow up without a father to help his mother. Or like now, when he ran because his sudden and all-encompassing reaction to Lee Ann Lawson had dominated his thoughts from the moment he'd met her.

He turned the bend and jogged in place on the corner while a lone car crossed in front of him before he sprinted across the intersection toward the park.

Mist was still on the leaves, and the earth was moist beneath his feet. The sun turned the horizon a brilliant orange as it rose above it all.

There were less than a handful of joggers in the park, some of the regulars who seemed to have the same pull to this moment of the morning as he did. He adjusted the earbuds of his iPod in his ears and started around the track, lifting his chin in acknowledgment to those he met along the way.

He wondered what Lee Ann did to unwind. He wondered what her first thought would be this morning when she awoke. He wondered if she thought something special had happened between them or if it was simply wishful thinking on his part and if she was as eager to see him later that afternoon as he was to see her.

They'd agreed to meet at Treme, a new bistro that had recently opened in downtown Baton Rouge. The service was said to be excellent and the food even better. He ran a little faster as if mentally pushing the day forward.

Back home he showered and changed into his college T-shirt from Loyola University and his favorite pair of khaki shorts that were frayed around the waist and hem from so many years of washing.

While he sipped his coffee and read the paper, he kept getting distracted by thoughts of Lee Ann. More than once he thought of calling her, just to say good morning. But it was barely 7:00 a.m. By ten o'clock, however, he couldn't wait any longer and pressed in her numbers on his cell phone.

Lee Ann was in her home office, reviewing and revising her father's calendar and planning his itinerary for the upcoming week. At sixty, Branford Lawson was still incredibly busy between his enormous responsibilities as senior senator and his social obligations. She tried to maintain an even balance for him and still factor in some time for family and relaxation.

But today she found it impossible to concentrate on a task that she could do with her eyes closed. That was the problem; every time she blinked she saw Preston, as she had throughout the night. And when her eyes opened with the sun, the images that had slept with her were so potent that she was stunned to realize that he was not there with her.

She reached for the phone on the desk, thinking of calling him but decided that was much too forward. What would he think? And at the same time that doubt entered the equation, her cell phone rang on the other side of the desk. She lifted it, and Preston's name and phone number appeared on the illuminated face. Hot air filled her lungs. She pressed Talk and hoped that she didn't sound as breathless as she felt.

"Hello…"

"Good morning. I hope this isn't too early."

His voice soothed her. She relaxed against the leather of her seat. "Not at all. I've been up for hours."

"Then I rescind my attempt at an unnecessary apology." Her laughter tinkled in his ears. "So other than dying to see me this afternoon, what are your plans for today?"

"At the moment I was going over my father's schedule and making a few adjustments here and there. At least it's only a few more grueling weeks before the Senate breaks for summer recess. But of course you know that already."

"True. I'm looking forward to it myself."

"Do you have plans for the break?"

"Hmm, I did, but I may change my mind about a few things. Let's talk about it over lunch."

"Sure."

"Well, I'll let you get back to work, and I'll find something to keep myself busy until I see you."

It wasn't so much what he said but the intonation of how he said it, with a stomach-fluttering sincerity that left her momentarily without words.

"One o'clock," she said.

"On the dot. See you later."

She disconnected the call but could still feel the pull of Preston's voice and couldn't wait to see him.

"Hey, Lee," Dominique said, tapping on her sister's bedroom door.

Lee Ann stepped out of her walk-in closet, holding up two of her favorite summer dresses. "Hi. Whatsup?" Her gaze and concentration drifted back and forth between peach and Mediterranean blue.

Dominique came in and plopped down on the end of Lee Ann's queen-size bed. "I was wondering if you could loan me a few bucks."

Lee Ann lowered the dresses and focused on her sister. "A few? How many is a few, and what for this time?"

"You don't have to say it like that," Dominique huffed, feigning offense.

Lee Ann crossed the room, undecided about her dresses and what to do about her sister. This was the third time in a month. "How much, Dom?"

"Five hundred."

Lee Ann's eyes widened, and her mouth opened then closed. "Dominique, what in the world for? I just gave you three less than a week ago."

Dominique sprang into an upright position on the

bed and put on her saddest, most earnest expression. "I know this sounds bad, but I maxed out my credit card and you know how hard I'm trying to keep a good credit rating so that I can get my own place without having to depend on you and Daddy."

Lee Ann cut a look at her sister's sorry attempt to win her over and rolled her eyes. She tossed the dresses onto the bed and stood over Dominique with her hands planted on her waist. "Listen, this cannot go on. It can't. You have a job, a hefty spending allowance and you still can't manage your money. You can't spend every dime you get on the latest fashions, girlfriend getaways and who knows what else!"

Dominique folded her arms beneath her full breasts, pushing them higher into view over her low cut, body hugging T-shirt. "That's so unfair. You know my job at the nonprofit barely covers my hair appointments."

"What you do is what's more important," Lee Ann chided. "Young, single, poor mothers come to you for help, and when they do that's worth much more than a paycheck."

"I know that. I do love my work, but personal satisfaction doesn't pay bills."

"Then don't accumulate them. Live within your means."

Dominique stood as if catapulted off the bed. They were at eye level. "Live within my means! We're rich for heaven's sake."

Dominique looked so astounded and bereft that Lee Ann seemed not to understand that fact, that Lee Ann did all but burst out laughing. Instead, she turned away to keep the laughter out of her eyes.

"I'll loan you three," she conceded. "You'll have to figure out how to get the rest. Go bug Rafe."

"Ooh, thank you, thank you," she said, wrapping her arms around her sister and kissing her on the cheek.

"I'll deposit the money into your account when I go out later."

It was then that Dominique noticed her sister was getting ready to go somewhere. She lifted one dress from the bed and then the other. "Where are you off to?"

"Out."

"Out where? With who? Anyone I know?"

"Out for brunch if you must know," she said, spinning out of her sister's web of questions.

Dominique eyed her with suspicion. "Why are you being so evasive? Why can't you just tell me where you're going? Suppose something happens to one of us or you. No one will know where you are. And don't you watch *The First 48?*" she added dramatically. "The first 48 hours are always crucial in an investigation."

Lee Ann held up her hand to stop the onslaught of Dominique. "All right, all right. I give up. But…don't read anything into it," she warned. "I'm having brunch with Senator Graham."

Dominique frowned for a moment, and then her eyes popped with excitement. "The gorgeous new Senator Graham, Daddy's protégé?"

"Yes."

"Well I'll be. Still waters. It's about damned time you went out on a date."

"It's not a date."

"Of course it is." She rocked her head from side

to side. "You aren't planning to spend the entire time talking business and politics as usual, are you?"

"I don't know what we'll talk about."

"Then it's a date!" she said triumphantly. "And since that's the case, you are not wearing the blue one. Peach is soft and feminine and brings out the color of your eyes." She held up the peach spaghetti strap dress that smoothed along the curves of Lee Ann's petite frame and stopped just above her knees.

"You think so?"

"I know so." She held the dress up in front of her. "And I have the perfect accessories." She shoved the dress at her sister and darted out of the room.

Moments later, she returned with Desiree in tow.

"You're going on a date with Preston Graham?" Desiree said as if he were a rock star. "That is so awesome. He's yummy. I didn't know you knew him like that."

"I don't," Lee Ann said. "It's just lunch."

"It's a date," Dominique said. "Don't listen to her."

For the next hour, her twin sisters fussed over her as if she was getting ready for her senior prom. By the time she was ready to leave, she was exhausted from their chatter and advice. You'd think she'd never been out with a man before in her life. She knew how to handle herself. After all, she was the oldest sister—although Dominique had all three women beaten in the men department.

The afternoon was hot and muggy. The umbrella of trees only gave the illusion of cool. She was thankful for her short hairdo that held up against the onslaught of Louisiana weather. She turned on the air conditioner full blast in her gunmetal-gray, two-seater Mercedes-Benz convertible. The color was custom-mixed for her, and it drove like a cloud. It was a gift to herself on her thirtieth birthday, three years earlier. She checked her GPS built into the dash and made the right turn then navigated her way along the narrow streets. She spotted Treme up ahead and drove into the parking lot behind the restaurant.

Nerves overtook her, racing her heart and making her legs feel weak as she drew closer to the entrance. She pulled in a long breath of calm, tugged the door open and stepped into the cool dimness.

"Good afternoon," the hostess greeted. "A table for one or are you meeting someone?"

"I am meeting someone, actually," she said, peering into the restaurant space and the tables dotted with afternoon diners. "I'm a bit early. I can wait at the bar."

"If you leave the name of your party, I can direct them to you when they arrive."

"Graham is his last name."

The hostess jotted it down. "I'll let him know as soon as he gets here."

"Thank you." She walked over to the bar and slid onto the stool.

"What can I get for you?" the female bartender asked.

"White wine spritzer," came the deep voice from behind her left shoulder.

Lee Ann slowly turned on the stool and looked up into his smiling face. Her heart banged in her chest, momentarily stunting her breath.

"Sorry to keep you waiting." He leaned down and placed a featherlight kiss on her cheek.

"Not at all. I just sat down."

"Next time we'll arrive together."

Next time, she thought. A happy bubble tumbled in her stomach.

"You want to sit here with your drink, or should we get a table now?"

"Let's get settled."

The bartender returned with the drink.

"Thanks. You can add this to our tab," Preston said, taking the drink and helping Lee Ann to her feet. "I got a table by the window just in case we get tired of talking to and looking at each other. We can then pretend to watch street traffic."

Lee Ann laughed, feeling the knots of anxiousness begin to loosen. "Very funny. But definitely an idea worth having."

"Although I can't imagine not wanting to look at and talk to you," he said. His voice drifted to her over her shoulder, the heat of his words warming her cheek and fanning out to her limbs. She glanced behind her for an instant to measure the sincerity of his voice with his eyes, but he was looking ahead and not at her.

Preston guided her to their table, and several heads turned in their direction as they crossed the restaurant, his face recognizable from the local papers and the news. He offered a casual nod but didn't stop. Lee Ann was thankful for that. She wanted this first time to be for them and not turn into a circus.

They came to their table, and Preston pulled out Lee Ann's chair for her then sat down. Once they were settled, he asked, "So…how have you been since the last time I saw you?"

Lee Ann chuckled. "I've been just fine, and you?"

"You have a great laugh, you know. Rich and honest."

She lowered her gaze for an instant. "Thank you."

Preston reached for his glass of water and took a slow sip, staring at her from above the rim, amazed with the way the golden flecks in her eyes picked up the daylight from outside—something he hadn't noticed last night—and the way the pulse in her throat beat and how her skin looked like honey, perfect and sweet to the taste.

"Is something wrong?" she asked breaking his trance.

He blinked and gave a slight shake of his head. "No, I'm sorry. I guess I was staring."

Lee Ann shifted in her seat.

He put down his glass and released a tight breath then leaned forward. His voice was low when he spoke. "Listen, I'm going to be honest because I like to be clear and up-front right from the beginning."

She nodded and waited for the shoe to fall.

"I rarely date. I don't have time. Because of my choice of careers, it's hard to have a lot of downtime or privacy. And coming from the family that you do, I'm sure you can understand that." He paused, started to speak then stopped and started again. "What I'm trying to say is I don't know what's going on in my head, and I know we've only met and you don't know any more about me than a stranger on the street. But I want to get to know you—Lee Ann the woman, not Branford

Lawson's daughter. And I want you to get to know me, Preston Graham—the guy with student loans, dishes in the sink and a Lab retriever named Rocky."

The tension that she felt burst into effervescent bubbles of laughter. "So, besides dirty dishes, student loans and a dog named Rocky, what else do I need to know about you?"

The afternoon went by much too fast, but over a light lunch of grilled chicken salad, several glasses of wine and raspberry sorbet for dessert, they talked and laughed and talked. Lee Ann discovered that they were both avid joggers. Preston was delighted to learn that Lee Ann was captain of her debate team in college and had also majored in political science. He was devoted to his mother, she to her father. His favorite book was James Baldwin's *Another Country*; hers was Emily Brontë's *Wuthering Heights*. They both loved New Orleans jazz and boasted about their collections. They were angered, appalled and frightened by the devastation along the Gulf Coast resulting from the catastrophic BP oil spill and the still unresolved devastation caused by Hurricane Katrina.

Preston took his last satisfying spoonful of sorbet. He glanced around Treme's and noticed that the clientele had changed several times since their arrival, and early dinner patrons were starting to drift in.

"I'm thinking they're going to actually ask us to leave if we don't do it on our own," Preston quipped.

Lee Ann ducked her head and took a cursory glance around, catching the eye of their empathetic waitress. "I think you're right."

He signaled for the waitress, who brought the bill. Preston paid the tab and ushered Lee Ann out into the sweltering early evening. It was almost after four.

"I didn't know it could take that long to eat a salad," Lee Ann joked. She slipped on her wide, dark sunglasses.

"Neither did I, but I enjoyed it."

She glanced at him as they walked to the parking lot. "So did I."

"Where are you parked?"

She pointed to her beloved car.

His brows rose in appreciation. "Very nice," he said, drawing out the two words.

"What about you?"

"The blue one over there," he said with a lift of his chin.

Lee Ann turned her gaze in that direction. "Oh, you mean the Jaguar over there," she said tongue in cheek.

Preston grinned.

"We'll have to swap rides one day. I've always wanted to get behind the wheel of a Jaguar."

"Anytime you're ready." He walked her to her car and waited while she opened the door.

She turned to him, and her heart did that thing again in her chest. "Thank you for a wonderful afternoon. Really."

"I'm glad you said yes. And if you're not busy tonight, I hope you'll say yes to doing something fun. There's a concert in the park. It starts at seven. Then the after-dark movie. It's always pretty good, something old and in black-and-white."

She blinked away her surprise. "Tonight? I… Yes, I'd like that."

"I'll pick you up at six-thirty. Will that give you enough time?"

"Sure, if I leave right this second."

They both laughed.

"I'll see you soon."

Lee Ann got in her car. Preston closed her door and waved before walking off to his. She sang off-key all the way home.

Chapter 3

Lee Ann darted into the house. She'd lost a lot of time getting back. There were some street closures from a protest rally by local merchants who'd lost their businesses as a result of the oil spill. Thousands of business owners were still waiting for checks, and now not only were their livelihoods at risk but their entire way of life and living, as well. It was an issue that plagued the people of the Gulf and across the United States. Her father was on the Gulf Coast Restoration Committee, so she kept abreast of the facts and fallacies of what was really going on.

She had one foot on the stairs when her father stepped out of his study on the ground floor.

"There you are."

Lee Ann stopped short, her hand on the oak banister. "Hi."

"I wanted to go over a few things with you about

this schedule." He read the pages in front of him from above his half-framed glasses. "We need to make some adjustments."

"Um, can it wait until morning?"

He pulled his glasses off and peered at his daughter. "Morning? You know I leave to go to Washington in the morning."

Briefly she shut her eyes then turned and walked toward her father. "Right. I wasn't thinking. Let me take a look."

"That's not like you," Branford said. "You generally don't miss things like that."

"I guess I wasn't thinking. I was in a little bit of a hurry this morning."

She walked into her father's study with him close on her heels. She turned on the computer and loaded the calendar information. Within moments, she located his itinerary for the upcoming month.

"Where did you want to make the adjustments, Daddy?"

He stood over her shoulder and pointed to the different dates on the calendar. "Next week Wednesday needs to change. And I can't have that meeting with the assembly tomorrow because I won't be here. I'm going to need you to make some phone calls and extend my apologies."

Lee Ann typed as her father talked, while thinking about her date with Preston. She could almost hear the clock ticking and her time to get ready running out. She made all the changes that her father requested, saved the file and then turned to him. "Anything else?" she asked.

"Well, you're mighty testy this evening. Something wrong?"

Lee Ann moved back from the desk and stood. She turned to her father and pushed a smile across her mouth. "No, nothing's wrong. Everything is fine. Why would you think that?"

"You seem a little jumpy. Like you don't have your mind on what you're doing."

"Well, I do have plans for the evening. And I'm running a little behind schedule."

Branford raised a questioning brow. "Plans? I don't recall you mentioning that you have plans for the evening."

"It just came up today." She began to walk toward the door and wondered why she didn't just tell her father that she was going out with Preston. She knew why. She didn't want her father's scrutiny, his acceptance or rejection—at least not tonight. She wanted to get through tonight.

"You're going to walk out and not say where you're going?" The idea was totally inconceivable to him.

Lee Ann turned back toward her father, suddenly feeling like a little girl instead of a 33-year-old woman. "I'm going out, Daddy. To a concert in the park."

For a moment, Branford looked as if he could not process the information. It was almost comical if it wasn't a testament to the kind of life her father perceived that she lived.

"I've really got to get ready." She hurried across the foyer and darted up the stairs to her room. Once she reached the bedroom, she went into her private bath and turned on the water full blast. While she stood under the pulsing water she went through a mental inventory of the things hanging in the closet wondering what would be appropriate to wear to a night in the park with a handsome young senator.

Wrapped in a towel, she paced in front of her walk-in closet looking for the perfect outfit. So much of her wardrobe was either formal or business attire, with a few casual outfits that she hadn't worn in much too long and her two favorite dresses—one of which he'd already seen her in and the other her sisters said did nothing for her. As she stood there, she was hit with the telling revelation that she had no *date* clothes—not even for a park date. Preston would be there in a half hour, and she was stuck in her closet with nothing to wear. This would never happen to Dominique. Dominique!

Lee Ann tugged the towel from around her body and put on her robe before dashing down the hallway to her sister's bedroom. She knocked. No answer.

"Looking for Dom?"

Lee Ann turned. Justin was coming up the stairs.

"She's out back."

"Thanks, sweetie." She breezed by him on the staircase and ran out to the garden behind the house.

Dominique was stretched out on a lounge chair with her iPod earbuds plugged in. Her eyes were closed, and she was rocking her foot to the rhythm playing in her head.

Lee Ann tapped her on the shoulder. Dominique lowered her sunglasses and looked up. She pulled the earbuds out. "Whatsup?" She looked her sister up and down.

"I really need your help. Like right now."

Dominique's thinly arched brows rose in surprise. She swiveled to an upright position. "*You* need my help?"

"Yes," she said through her teeth. She grabbed Dominique's hand and tugged her off the veranda and upstairs. "Come on. He'll be here any minute."

"Who?"

"Preston," Lee Ann tossed over her shoulder.

Dominique beamed. "Well, all righty then. That's what I'm talking about. How can I help?"

"I need something to wear." They reached the landing, and Lee Ann led the way to Dominique's room.

"Well, you've come to the right place."

They entered Dominique's dressing room, which could have been an easy substitute for the main floor of a high-end boutique. Lee Ann knew that Dominique had a passion for clothes—expensive clothes and shoes and bags—but she had no idea to what extent her passion had grown. Her mouth dropped open as she followed Dominique along the expanse of her closet. It was actually an adjacent room that had been converted to accommodate her wardrobe, which could easily clothe a small neighborhood, Lee Ann thought in awe, and that was with the clothes that still had tags on them. She had to give it to her sister though. Dominique did her fair share of donating. A great percentage of her brand-new clothing went to the nonprofit of which she was the executive director. First Impressions provided clothing and job preparation training for women who had been out of the job market because of prison, homelessness or prior drug problems. That was the other side of her sister that most people didn't know about.

Dominique spun toward her sister, hands on her hips. "So, what kind of date is it? Is it fabulously chic, stuffy formal, fashionably casual or simply naughty?" she added with a wink.

"We're going to the concert in the park and then staying for the movie."

Dominique pursed her lips. "Fashionably casual." She walked to the far end of the closet. "I've been telling you for years that you need to diversify your wardrobe." She pressed her finger to her lips. "Hmm." She plucked a pair of salmon-colored cotton slacks that stopped at the midcalf with a cuff. She pulled a variety of multicolored sleeveless tops, some with swooping necklines, V-necks, layered in sheer fabric over something silky. She pulled out accessories—belts, earrings, purses, necklaces—and carried her treasures to the bed. "Any of these tops will do," she said with authority. "The key, as I've always said, is the accessories, the magic ingredient."

Lee Ann did a quick scan of the tops and plucked one from the group. "This will be fine." She took the slacks.

Dominique selected silver accessories and a clutch Coach purse in the same color as the slacks and handed her a shrug sweater that picked up the pale green in the top.

"Thanks, sis." She hurried toward the door, with Dominique on her heels.

"Anytime. If he gets here before you're ready, I'll keep him busy."

Lee Ann glanced back at her sister. Dominique was a man magnet. She drew them to her with little effort on her part beyond simply breathing. She tugged in a breath. "Sure. Thanks." She hurried off to her room and got dressed.

Her plan was to be ready and waiting for him on the front porch so that they could bypass the family interrogation. She knew her family meant well. They could just be a bit overwhelming to some people, especially when they all converged on you at once.

That wasn't her biggest issue, she thought, as she checked her lipstick and dropped it into her purse. Her real issue was she was totally out of practice. She hadn't been on a "date" that wasn't business related since she and Maxwell Harris broke up. She'd been devastated. He claimed it wasn't her, that he just needed some space to find himself. He found himself, all right, married to Ashley Montgomery six months later. Lee Ann was humiliated. Max was the first man she loved, right out of college. She thought he was the one. Unfortunately, he didn't feel the same way.

Right after that, her mother grew ill, and Lee Ann threw herself into taking care of her. It helped them both. Louisa drew a kind of strength from Lee Ann. And Lee Ann was able to pour all of her love and attention into her mother and push aside all thoughts of Maxwell. That was five years ago, and she hadn't been "involved" with anyone since—a date here and there but nothing serious. Between looking after her father's affairs and taking care of her family, there wasn't time. At least that's what she told herself.

Lee Ann took her house keys and cell phone from the dresser, added them to the contents of her purse and went downstairs just as her brother Rafe was coming through the door with Preston in tow.

"Look who I found lurking out front." He clapped Preston on the back.

Lee Ann landed on the last step and approached the devastatingly handsome duo. She leaned up and kissed her brother's cheek. "Hi." She turned to Preston. "I hope he didn't say anything out of the way, which he's prone to do without warning." She cut Rafe a playful look.

"You wound me, dear sister." He winked. "I didn't get the chance to run him through the mill, so where are you two headed?"

"Concert in the park," Preston offered.

Rafe frowned. He looked from one to the other. "A political concert?"

"No," Lee Ann said simply. "We should go, Preston. We'll be late."

"Right. Good seeing you again, Rafe."

Rafe murmured something unintelligible just as Branford emerged from his study. "Preston?"

Preston turned. "Hello, Senator Lawson."

Branford slowly approached, taking in the scene. Lee Ann wanted to disappear.

"Did we have an appointment?" He frowned at Lee Ann, while shaking Preston's hand.

"No, sir, we didn't."

"Then I don't understand…"

"Preston is here to see me, Daddy, and we're late." She turned and walked to the door.

"To see you?" He glared from one to the other. "What in heaven's name for?"

"We were—"

Lee Ann cut Preston off. "Goodnight, daddy." She walked to the door and stepped out.

"Good night, everyone," Preston said, not really sure what scenario was being played out. He closed the door behind them and followed Lee Ann down the steps and to his waiting car. Tonight it was the Lexus SUV.

"I'm really sorry about that," Lee Ann murmured. Preston opened the car door for her.

"You want to tell me what's going on? Is there something that I should know?"

"Only that my family is…close for lack of a better word. *Too* close at times." She fastened her seat belt.

Preston got in behind the wheel and turned the key in the ignition. "I think it's nice."

She glanced at him, and the warm, sincere smile of understanding unraveled the knot that had tightened in her stomach.

He put the car in gear and drove out of the winding driveway. "I get the impression that you're really important to them—at least from what I've seen."

"Really?"

"Not to mention how highly your father speaks of you as often as he can." His flashed an amused smile.

"Hmm, I don't know. I think it's more of a comfort than anything else."

"A comfort? Why do you say that?"

She was thoughtful for a moment before she began to speak about those days that were still painful to remember. "When my mother got sick, it seemed natural to me to take care of her, being the oldest daughter." Her voice drifted as the memories of those difficult days pushed to the forefront. "My father, as strong as he is in front of the country, couldn't handle the thought of losing his wife. His visits to her sickbed often did them both more damage than good. Telling him he had to be strong for her usually resulted in a firestorm of outrage—how could he be expected to be strong when the most important person in his life was being taken from him? Dom and Desi spent most of their time crying or moaning about how unfair it was. Rafe was like a ghost in those days. He was her favorite. They were so close," she said softly. "And Justin, to be the youngest, he was a real trooper. I don't know what I would have done without him." She sighed. "I guess I took over where my mother left off—taking care of the house, the staff and the family." She glanced at him. "I'm sorry. I didn't mean to go on and on."

"Please." He stretched his hand across the gears and covered hers. "It's fine."

"I made them sound so awful and selfish. They really aren't."

Preston chuckled. "You did make the whole crew sound like a bunch of brats," he teased. "Except for Justin."

Lee Ann ducked her head for a moment and bit back a grin. "They're really quite sweet."

"I'm sure." He paused a moment before making the turn toward the park entrance. "I, uh, got the impression that they—your father and brother—didn't know about us and tonight."

Her face heated. "No, they didn't."

He bobbed his head. "Any reason?"

"I'm not really sure what the reason was," she said a bit more harshly than she'd intended. "I just didn't tell them." She tightened her grip around her purse.

Preston's brow arched for a moment, and he knew

to back off. Whatever her reason was, it was her own. But he didn't have the time or the inclination to tiptoe around anyone. He'd never done it in his life and had no intention of starting now.

He drove the car as far as he could and then found a parking space. "We'll have to walk from here. It's not far," he said. "Right up the ridge and down on the other side."

Lee Ann nodded. Preston came around and helped her out of the car. Gone was the easy, excited feeling, replaced with the rubber bands of tension that had popped between them during their first meeting at the reception.

Preston took a blanket from the trunk and tucked it under his arm. "This way," he muttered and jutted his chin. Lee Ann fell in step beside him.

He was annoyed, he realized as they walked in side-by-side silence. Annoyed at the one thing he promised he would not allow himself to be ever again—how someone else's agenda affected him. But he held his tongue. One night. The last night. Move on.

They reached the top of the ridge, and from that vantage point, the multicolored quilt of the crowd splashed out before them. One of the bands was already on stage and launched into their first number.

Preston instinctively took Lee Ann's hand as they maneuvered their way across the uneven landscape and around bodies in search of a piece of space, and against his own steely determination, the sensation of her fingers wrapped around his hand seemed to soothe the ache that always resided inside him.

"Looks like a spot over there," Lee Ann said, in

a voice that carried a soft echo of sadness that gave Preston pause.

He gave her hand a little squeeze. Her eyes slid up to his face then pulled away.

"Let's grab it before someone else does."

They walked faster and just beat out another couple thanks to Preston's quick work of staking their claim with the almost theatrical unfurling of the blanket, which reminded Lee Ann of a matador teasing the oncoming bull. She told him as much once they'd sat down.

"A matador?" Preston laughed a deep, tumbling laugh that broke the tenuous band of tension between them. He looked at her soft, smiling face and settled down beside her. "I've been called a lot of things, but I think matador is a first. I kind of like it though."

He grinned, flashing that sexy smile that lit his eyes and stole her breath away.

Preston reached out and tenderly touched the wisps of dark hair that feathered her brow. He moved a bit closer. Lee Ann's heart began to race.

The crowd burst into thunderous applause as the band finished their number.

Lee Ann blinked as if awakened from a light sleep. Preston gave an imperceptible shake of his head.

"I...uh, didn't think to bring snacks," Lee Ann blurted out in that odd moment of awkwardness.

Preston slapped his brow with the heel of his palm. "Oh man, I left them in the car." He sprang to his feet. "I'll be right back. Hold my spot," he added with a wink. He jogged back the way they had come and was soon swallowed by the throng.

Lee Ann sat with her legs tucked beneath her and took a look around, while she ran through her head that push and pull that kept happening between her and Preston. Granted, she was no expert on dating or the prelude to it, but she had good plain sense and always relied on her instincts. But for reasons that she couldn't put her finger on, Preston, at the slightest instance, would retreat to a space and cut her out, almost in retribution. Maybe it was the bump in the road of getting to know each other. Maybe she was making more out of it than necessary. Maybe it was just her imagination. Whatever it was, she wasn't sure she knew how to deal with it or if she wanted to.

Preston opened the back door of the car and retrieved the compact blue-and-white cooler that he'd left on the floor. If he'd had his head in the right place instead of taking a detour down that dark road, he wouldn't have forgotten. He needed to get over it. The past was the past. Lee Ann was not part of that space in his life. He shut the door and used his key alarm to lock the car.

"Preston?"

A jolt went through him. He turned in the direction of the familiar voice.

"It is you." She walked over to him, leaving the man she was with looking at her swaying hips. She stopped in front of him and let her eyes trail over his face for an instant before she placed a featherlight kiss on his cheek. She used the pad of her thumb to wipe away the imprint of her cherry-red lipstick. "How have you been? Congratulations are in order," she said in that throaty drawl that used to drive him wild.

"I've been fine. Thanks." His jaw clenched.

She puckered her lips for a moment. "It's been a long time, Press."

He could feel the heat rising off her body, her scent slipping beneath his clothing. Her nipples jutted against the thin fabric of her shirt, boldly announcing her bralessness.

"I have to go. Good seeing you, Charlotte." He started to move around her. She clasped his arm.

"I miss you," she said in a hungry whisper. "Every day."

Preston jerked his chin in the direction of her companion. "Your friend is waiting for you." He glanced down at the hand that held his arm, and the diamond flashed beneath the street lights. "You plan on leaving him at the altar, too?"

She flinched. Her expression shifted from hot to cold. "I made a mistake. We were young."

He stared down into her ivy-green eyes. His voice was low and laden with apathy. "It doesn't matter anymore." He pulled away from her hold and walked away, casting a sidelong glance at the man who must be her new fiancé.

Preston stood at the top of the ridge. He looked back to where he'd just come. The sunny Sunday afternoon six years earlier stood before him. Instead of marrying the woman he'd loved he got a note from her cousin. She couldn't do it. She wasn't ready. She was sorry. That was it. It was over. It was six years ago, but seeing Charlotte like that brought it all back. He trotted down the slope then wound his way around the sprawled and propped up bodies until he reached Lee Ann.

Her back was turned to him, and he took the moment to pull himself together. He knew that part of his recalcitrant behavior was due to what happened to him years ago and finding out several months later the real reason for Charlotte's betrayal. He wasn't good enough, and she wasn't going to wait around for his career to "take off." His jaw tightened. But like all the obstacles and defeats that had faced him throughout his life, he took that and used it as a springboard to get him where he was today, a U.S. senator.

Preston drew in a breath and crossed the rest of the distance to Lee Ann.

"Got it," he said, dropping down beside her.

She turned her engaging smile on him, and it seemed as if in the time that he was gone, the tight thin line between her brow was gone, her shoulders seemed softer and her body was relaxed. He hoped that if it was he who had drawn the line and tightened her shoulders and body that he would have the chance to see and get to know the Lee Ann in front of him now.

"I've never heard Spyro Gyra live. They're fabulous." Her eyes sparkled.

He winked. "Told ya it would be great." He pulled open the top of the cooler and pulled out a bottle of wine and a tray of crackers, cheese and fruit.

"Wow, I am totally impressed." She plucked a grape from the stem.

He uncorked the bottle and poured the white wine into a clear plastic cup for Lee Ann and one for himself.

He held up his cup and tapped it against hers. "To giving each other a chance."

Lee Ann looked into the depths of his eyes. "I like that."

Chapter 4

By the time Lee Ann and Preston pulled into the Lawson driveway, it was well past 1:00 a.m. Lee Ann couldn't remember the last time she'd had so much fun on such a simple outing—wine, cheese and fruit in the park.

Preston had been nothing but charming, funny, knowledgeable and downright sexy all night long. He had a running string of jokes about the members of the education committee that he sat on that had her laughing so hard she caught a cramp in her side that he eagerly massaged away, only to begin on another campaign to double her over.

She could barely pay attention to the movie, *Breakfast at Tiffany's*, for his tales about Senator Carter's love-child scandal were much more entertaining.

"I had a wonderful time," she said when they came

to a stop. "Thanks. I can't remember the last time I laughed so hard."

Preston grinned and turned off the engine. "I had a good time, too." He lowered his gaze and paused for a moment then looked into her eyes "I want to apologize if I was…out of sorts earlier."

She offered a tight-lipped smile. "Me, too."

"I hope tonight will be the first of many for us."

Her face heated. "So do I," she said softly.

Preston held her in place with the darkness of his eyes until his face blurred and the soft, sweet pressure of his lips touched hers.

She drew in a breath as warmth spread through her body and turned it to hot liquid.

His mouth moved slowly over hers, willing her lips to part. And when the tip of his tongue grazed her pliant lips, a jolt of electricity shot through them both.

Involuntarily, Preston groaned deep in his throat and thread his fingers through her hair to ease her deeper into the kiss. Lee Ann willingly let him enter and did a slow sensual dance with him. She pressed her hands against his shoulders and squeezed, feeling as if she was floating and needing the solidness of him for support. Her heart hammered. Blood rushed to her head and pounded then rushed to her limbs, settling between her thighs and beating like a tiny drum.

The flood of oncoming headlights filled the car and pulled them apart. The roar of Rafe's motorcycle ebbed then came to a rumbling stop behind them.

Preston and Lee Ann gave each other the look of two teens caught necking.

Rafe hopped off his bike and came around to the driver's side and peeked in.

Preston depressed the window button, and it slowly eased down.

"Hey," Rafe greeted, looking from one to the other.

"Hi," Lee Ann said, totally embarrassed.

"Rafe," Preston said simply.

"Just getting in?" Rafe asked.

"We went to a concert in the park," Lee Ann offered.

"Hmm. Well, don't mind me," he said with a wicked grin. "Take it easy, man. Nice ride," he added before trotting up the steps to the front door.

Preston lowered his head and chuckled. "Can't remember the last time that happened." He angled his head and peeked at Lee Ann, and they both burst out laughing.

"I probably should go," she said over her laughter.

"Not just yet." He slipped his arm around her waist and pulled her as close as their separate seats would allow. "When can I see you again?"

"When do you want to see me again?"

"Tomorrow."

She drew in a breath. "Okay. Anything special?"

"Let's play it by ear. I'll call you."

She nodded then turned to open the car door.

He pulled her back and took her mouth again, searing her lips with his heat in a long, deep kiss that had them both reeling. Reluctantly, he moved back and let his eyes roam over her face. "I wanted to leave you with something to remember me by until I see you again."

"I think you succeeded, but I'll let you know when

I see you later." She smiled and got out of the car. She looked back once before disappearing inside.

Preston sat in the car for a few minutes to get his mind and body together before pulling off into the night.

He knew he wasn't going to be able to sleep from the moment he set foot in his house. He walked into his living room and turned on his sound system to his favorite jazz station. Then he fixed himself a tumbler of bourbon. Relaxing on the couch, he put his feet up and sipped his drink, going over in his mind his evening with Lee Ann.

He hadn't expected to be so completely taken by her. A part of him had made up his mind to just go through the motions and call it a night. But there was something about Lee Ann beyond his attraction to her. She was beautiful, smart and incredibly sexy in an understated way, and he knew deep in his gut that she possessed a passion that was waiting to be released. He felt it when he touched her, when he looked into her eyes, the way she breathed, laughed, the way she kissed him with a raw urgency that denied her conservative demeanor. The combination was unsettling and caught him off balance.

Since Charlotte, he'd been totally driven and focused on his career. Of proving to himself and to Charlotte that he was the man he knew he could be. The man she walked out on. Women came and went. They were more for entertainment than any kind of commitment. He had no plans of being committed to anyone again. Charlotte had fixed that.

Now here, when he least expected it, Lee Ann Lawson came into his life.

He took another long swallow of his drink. It would be easy to fall into that trap again, allow his emotions to outweigh his objectives. He finished off his drink and set down the glass. He couldn't let that happen again—not even for a desirable woman like Lee Ann. Seeing Charlotte tonight only reinforced that for him.

He pushed up from the couch and climbed the stairs to his bedroom.

Lee Ann was getting undressed, still floating on the high of her evening. She could still feel the sweet pressure of Preston's lips on her mouth. Dreamily, she touched her lips with the tip of her finger, and her eyes drifted closed, just as there was a light knock on her door.

She went to the door and opened it. Dominique and Desiree were standing there all grins.

"Can I help you, ladies?" she asked, deadpan.

"You can let us in, for starters," Dominique said.

Lee Ann huffed in amusement and stepped aside to let them in. Thankfully, she didn't see Rafe again after she'd come in, but she couldn't slip under her sisters' radar. "It's late."

"Exactly," Desiree said, sitting on the edge of Lee Ann's bed. "So…spill it. What happened?"

"Nothing," she said innocently as she crossed the room to her lounge chair and picked up the clothes she'd had on earlier. She caught a whiff of Preston's scent. She put them back down and turned to her inquisitioners.

"You really want us to believe that nothing happened

from the time you left until now?" Dominique said. "Not even a peck on the cheek?"

Lee Ann blew out a breath. "All right, you beat it out of me," she teased and plopped down on the bed between the twins. "We had a wonderful time," she said wistfully, grinning from ear to ear. She recounted their evening, all the fun they had, their conversation up to Rafe pulling up behind them in the driveway. She left out the kiss.

"I could have strangled him," Lee Ann said, shaking her head.

Dominique snickered. "Who do you think told us to come here and get the scoop?"

Lee Ann's eyes widened. "I guess Justin will be next," she moaned. She threw them both a warning glance. "And don't either of you dare tell Rafe a thing!"

They both mirrored each other, miming zipping their lips.

Lee Ann popped up. "Now good night. Go."

"I still think you're holding something back," Dominique said as she walked to the door. "No way a man looking like Preston Graham, utterly edible, would just drop you off and say good-night."

Desiree hooked her arm through her twin sister's arm. "Let Lee have her moment. Come on. You are so nosy."

"I'm nosy!" Dominique protested. "Am I here by myself? You wanted to know as much as I did."

"You dragged me."

"Dragged you!"

Lee Ann pushed them both out of the door, laughing

at their antics as they continued their sisterly fussing all the way back to their rooms.

Lee Ann shut the door. She slowly shook her head. She loved her family. She really did. But sometimes…

As usual, when Branford was heading to Washington, the household was a flurry of activity. One would think that he was going off to battle the way he doled out orders, checked and rechecked information that Lee Ann had made available to him days in advance.

"I need you to be in the local office and check on the staff. There are quite a few local initiatives that are coming up in the next few weeks, and I don't want anything to slip through the cracks. The town hall meeting next week on the rezoning for downtown is coming up. You need to be there," Branford instructed for the third time.

"I know, Daddy. I'll be there." She put the files in his briefcase. "I went over your presentation for the Education Committee and added some additional statistics."

He nodded and shrugged into his jacket. "And I want you to have a talk with Dominique. I took a look at her credit card bill. What in the hell is that girl trying to do, run me into the poorhouse? Take care of it, Lee Ann."

"I will, Daddy. Stop worrying. I have everything under control."

"And Rafe…" He couldn't find the words. "I've been hearing rumors about some woman he's been seeing. A hostess at that…that club he keeps running off to. I won't tolerate another scandal from that boy."

"He's not a boy, Daddy. He's a grown man," she said as gently as she could. She adjusted his tie and brushed the shoulders of his jacket.

"Then he should act like one! Running around town on that bike. What kind of image is that?"

Lee Ann bit back a smile. Her father and Rafe stayed at odds. Branford wanted Rafe groomed to take over his Senate seat one day. And Rafe did everything in his power to drive his father insane, and she was constantly caught in the middle of the battle. Their egos were too big to be contained, and their historic explosions rattled the rafters for days on end.

Lee Ann ushered her father to the door. "Your driver is waiting. You're going to miss your flight."

He huffed and strode out into the foyer. He reached the door then turned to Lee Ann. "I'm depending on you," he said before kissing her forehead.

Lee Ann nodded and stood in the open doorway as he got into the waiting limo. She waited until the car pulled off before she closed the door and took a relieved breath.

She returned to the home office and took a quick look around. Granted she had a busy week ahead between her teaching job at Louisiana State University and her work at her father's office. But Sunday was going to be her day. A tingle rippled up her spine as the memory of Preston bloomed inside of her. She couldn't wait to see him and wondered what he'd planned for the day.

Preston opened the door to his house, wiping his dripping face with a towel. It was barely 10:00 a.m. and already the temperature was in the mid-eighties.

He should have gone for his run much earlier, but he'd overslept after finally dozing off near daybreak.

When he finally fell into a fitful sleep, his dreams were plagued with images of the day at the altar, the anguish and humiliation that he felt. The murmurs of condolences and speculation. The days and weeks that followed. He'd worked hard in the ensuing years to rid every fiber of his being of memories of Charlotte. But seeing her last night brought it all rushing back, and as much as he wanted and had been partially successful in banishing her from his head by focusing all of his attention on Lee Ann, the old wound had opened.

He tossed the damp towel on the bathroom floor and turned the shower on full blast. Stripping out of his clothing, he stepped under the water. And then to find a voice message from her on his house phone when he finally woke up and checked his messages had sent him deeper into the place that he'd worked so hard to escape. She wanted to see him, to talk. She left her cell phone number and pleaded with him to call her, no matter what time of day. "Just please call," she'd said in that same throaty whisper that used to singe his blood with desire.

Preston held his face up to the water and let it splash over him, wishing that it had the power to wash the past away. He turned off the water and stepped out of the shower stall. He wrapped a towel around his waist, draped a smaller one around his neck and went to his bedroom. He sat on the edge of the bed and reached for the phone just as it rang. It was Senator Lawson's private number.

"Senator Lawson, good morning."

"Good morning. I take it that I didn't wake you."

"No. Not at all. What can I do for you?"

"I'm at the airport. Heading back to Washington."

"Yes, sir, for the committee hearings."

"That's not why I'm calling."

Preston waited.

"This is about Lee Ann."

"Sir?"

"I'm sure you're a decent young fellow, and I have an enormous amount of respect for you as a colleague. But these are important times we are in. A time when we need to have our eyes on the prize—for the American people." He cleared his throat. "Very often we have to make personal sacrifices for the greater good."

Preston grew more irate as the implications of what Branford was saying began to take hold and materialize.

"I have an equal amount of respect for you, sir," he said through a tight jaw. "As such, I would never be presumptuous enough to infer that you allowed your personal wants or desires to cloud your political judgment or infringe on your career and your constituents, and I would hope that you feel the same way about me, sir," he added with emphasis.

"And as a savvy politician, though a young one, I'm sure that you fully understand what I'm telling you. Remember, you need friends in this business of ours."

Preston gripped the phone in astonished fury. He knew better than to say what was really on his mind, which was "go to hell," even as the senator virtually gripped him by the short hairs.

"I'll see you on the Hill on Tuesday."

The call disconnected.

Preston was so furious his head pounded. The senator had all but threatened him. The underlying implication was crystal clear—stay away from Lee Ann.

He tossed the cordless phone across the bed and rubbed his face with the towel from his neck. He stalked across the room then back again. He stared at the phone, replaying the conversation in his head. His eyes tightened into slits. Whatever intention he had of leaving Lee Ann alone was no longer an option. It was off the table. No one told him how to run his life—not even Senator Lawson.

Preston went back to the bed and snatched up the phone. He punched in Lee Ann's number to solidify their plans for the day.

Senator Lawson boarded the jet to Washington, taking his first-class seat. Settled, he snapped open the newspaper, calm and satisfied that his agenda, as always, was clear. He snorted a dry laugh. The boy wouldn't know what hit him.

Chapter 5

They drove into New Orleans shortly after noon with the intention of spending the day together. Preston had made reservations for the African Princess cruise ship, and they had lunch sailing leisurely along the Mississippi to the backdrop of the balmy spring air and the rhythm of a live jazz band.

"The fishing and tourist industry is still reeling from the oil spill," Lee Ann said as they sipped wine on the top deck.

"Even after all these months." He leaned against the railing. "It's going to take time and money. A lot of it. It's one of the issues I intend to tackle in the coming session. Not enough has been done. Life on the Gulf has been altered forever." He stared out along the horizon toward a future that her father wanted to infringe upon. He turned to Lee Ann. A flicker of a smile lifted the corners of his mouth. He stroked her cheek with the tip of his finger.

"When will you be going back to Washington?"

He stepped closer to her. She could feel his heat invade her body. "Tuesday for about three weeks. There are several bills that are up for review and a vote."

Her voice wavered. "The education reform bill?"

Preston nodded, searched her face for an instant before kissing her, suddenly possessed by a power greater than his will. It was slow and sweet, and he didn't care who was looking. A moan grumbled in his throat as desire began to pulse, trapped behind a thin zipper, and he stepped back, stared at her as if she was the power that broke his will and it shook him.

He took a sip of wine, cleared his throat and put them both back on solid ground. "It's important to the president to get this passed. If he's going to be effective in his second term, he has to come out swinging with a major win just like he did with health care and Wall Street reform."

Lee Ann nodded numbly, dreamlike, the upending sensation of wanting him clouding her thoughts. Had he not been holding her as they walked down the steps to the lower deck, she was sure she would have never found her way. They returned to their table.

"It always baffled me," Lee Ann said, finally finding her voice, as Preston helped her into her seat, "how anyone in their right mind could be against funding education for our children. It is such a no-brainer."

Preston grinned. "No-brainer is the operative word." He leaned back in his seat. "The ones making the decisions, for the most part, never missed a meal in their lives." His features hardened along with the timbre of his voice. "They have trust funds, their kids go to private schools. They have no idea what it means to struggle and settle. They come from money and make more of it and remain out of touch with the everyday person."

"Which is what cinched the presidency. He spoke to the everyday person. The ones who have been overlooked and made them really believe that they were the solution that the world was waiting for and that what they felt and wanted made a difference."

"Hmm, and how soon we forget," Preston said, the sarcasm not lost on Lee Ann.

She nodded slowly in agreement. "And how you beat an incumbent," she added, a note of admiration in her voice.

His laugh was self-deprecating. "Right time, right place. The voters were ready for a change." He focused on the band, knowing that if he concentrated his attention on Lee Ann he was liable to do something really stupid, like slip his hand under her dress or find a secluded spot on the boat and seduce her. It was crazy. His brain was on scramble—or rather his libido. Whatever the case, Lee Ann was at the root of it, and he didn't like it one bit.

Lee Ann's eyes strolled across the angles of his face, the contours and valleys. There was a resoluteness about Preston, from his countenance to his actions. She knew deep inside that once he made up his mind about something that was it; there was no changing it. So when the conversation turned to the coastline and what the government was doing, Lee Ann found herself spending the rest of the afternoon with Preston inspecting the wetlands that had been decimated by the oil and visiting some of the local businesses that were struggling to hang on. Even though it was Sunday, Preston was on the phone with one of his colleagues as he relayed what he saw, and they discussed some additional strategies that he would get into more detail about when he returned to Washington.

Lee Ann quietly observed it all and felt a new level of admiration for Preston, who didn't have a camera crew with him or reporters trailing behind him waiting for a sound bite. For him, this was personal, and he didn't need the glare of lights and a bouquet of microphones to do what he felt was important. She could tell that he was driven by his gut instincts, which could easily be a blessing or a curse.

"I really appreciate you coming out here," Preston said as they walked back to his car. "Trust me, it was not on the agenda or my idea of 'the perfect Sunday date,'" he teased. "When we started talking it got me all stirred up again." And he needed to defuse some of his pent-up sexual energies, he thought but didn't say. "I hadn't been out there in a few weeks. I like to know firsthand what's going on."

"No need to apologize. It was certainly an eye-opener for me. I've been watching from a distance. But to see and feel it up close…" Her voice drifted off.

"I feel like I need to make it up to you somehow."

They stopped in front of his Lexus.

She glanced up at him. A mischievous smile brimmed around his mouth. "Make it up to me?"

He put his arms around her waist and slowly drew

her flush against him. Lee Ann's sharp intake of breath lodged in the center of her chest when the full, hard line of his body found all the dips and curves of hers.

"How about I make us dinner on the grill, we lounge by the pool, listen to some music, talk, eat…maybe watch the sun come up?"

Her heart banged in her chest, and warmth flooded her body. The pads of his thumbs caressed her spine. She forced herself to breathe.

"Sounds wonderful." She ran her tongue across her bottom lip. "Why don't we play it by ear? See how it goes, where it takes us, how it feels?" she said with more calm than she knew she possessed.

Preston's eyes darkened with amused pleasure. "By ear it is." He opened the door for her and helped her in.

Lee Ann's fingers shook as she fastened her seat belt. She took a steadying breath as Preston hopped in behind the wheel. He gave her a quick look and a wink before turning on the engine.

"Hope you like hot dogs. It's the only thing I'm good at grilling."

Lee Ann looked at him and burst out laughing. "You are kidding, right?"

He made a face. "I toss a mean salad…"

She laughed harder. "Then I guess it's hot dogs and salad," she said over her giggles.

Preston's poker face split into a grin. "Now that's the kind of woman a man can roll with—someone who still cares even if a romantic night under the stars is celebrated with hot dogs and salad."

"You are a mess," she said, wiping her eyes.

"And just for your faith and willingness, I'll make a confession."

"Now what?"

"Actually, I have a freezer full of top-shelf steak, chicken and jumbo shrimp…and hot dogs," he said with a chuckle. "And I can't wait to show you all of my skills." He leaned across the gears and gently touched her lips with his before pulling out of the parking space and heading to his town house.

"Welcome, and make yourself comfortable," Preston said, opening the door and ushering Lee Ann in. Rocky hopped up from his throne near the couch and padded over to Preston then sniffed at Lee Ann's feet.

"He likes you," Preston said.

Lee Ann rustled his fur. "He's beautiful."

"Spoiled, too. Come on in."

Lee Ann followed Preston inside with Rocky trotting behind them. Her wide, light brown eyes took in the totally masculine space, and oddly she felt immediately at home as if she'd been here before. The decor was a rich chocolate, the couches and chairs looking as if they'd been whisked to heavenly lightness. She couldn't guess the size of the enormous television that dominated the room, and his sound system surely required an engineering degree. Yet, it was comfortable and welcoming. Magazines were tossed on the wood and glass tables, and she noticed a pair of sneakers peeking out from the side of the club chair and a lone jacket tossed across the top.

She followed him through the open living room to the kitchen that led to the backyard. Preston pulled open the sliding glass doors and stepped outside. The enclosed yard was like an oasis. A large peach tree gave shade as well as additional privacy. The flooring was terra-cotta in a bronze color with inlaid lighting. But it was the kidney-shaped pool that was the centerpiece. Lounge chairs dotted the perimeter.

"This is fabulous," she said.

"Thanks. I wish I could make more use of it than I do." He walked over to a small bar. "Can I fix you something to drink?"

"Sure." She crossed the cool stones to where he stood.

"How about a Fuzzy Navel?" he asked with a grin.

"That was my mother's favorite drink."

"With or without vodka?"

"With."

He prepared and mixed the ingredients of peach schnapps, orange juice, lemonade and Absolut Vodka; added some ice; and poured her a glass. "Tell me what you think."

She brought the glass to her lips and took a small sip. "Hmm. Perfect."

"Great. Well, you relax, I'm going to check the freezer and get dinner started. I promised to show you my skills."

"Yes, you did."

"Be right back."

Lee Ann took her drink and settled down on one of the lounge chairs. She felt totally at ease even as a thread of excitement continued to run through her veins. She intended to go with the flow and let the evening take its course. Tonight, she was going to put the issues of everyone else aside and concentrate on Lee Ann—for once. She sipped her drink, allowing the sweet fruit and hint of liquor to flow through her, unwind her even further. She closed her eyes and listened to the sound of the birds harmonizing in the trees. Her insides smiled.

"Don't relax too much."

Lee Ann opened her eyes to see Preston standing above her with a large tray in his hands. He'd changed into a pair of khaki shorts and a T-shirt that stretched across the expanse of his hard chest. Her heart thumped in response.

"It's wonderful out here. Let me help you." She got up and went with him to the side of the yard where a grill fit for a football team stood.

They worked side by side seasoning the meat and cutting up the condiments.

"I can't let you in on the secret of my secret sauce," he teased.

"I swear I won't tell."

He shook his head. "Can't take that chance. It's my personal recipe." He turned on the grill. "So you go on over there out of the way while I get it together." He shooed her away and turned his back to her.

Lee Ann pretended to pout and sauntered over to her chair and finished her drink while Preston worked his magic.

"We'll let the meat marinate for a few while the grill is heating up," he said, joining her shortly after.

"What other secrets do you have?"

He stretched out on the chair and crossed his feet at the ankle. "Now if I told you that, it wouldn't be a secret anymore." He took a swallow from his drink and winked at her. "But I will tell you something that won't be a secret much longer."

"What's that?"

He leaned closer to her. "I intend to make this an evening that you will never forget."

"Promise," she asked on a breath.

"You have my word."

The next few hours Preston and Lee Ann ate and drank and talked and laughed and touched and shared light teasing kisses. He'd turned on the stereo system and Luther, John Legend, Maxwell and Anita Baker floated to them through the speakers hidden around the yard. They danced and touched and kissed some more. The moon hung at a precarious angle above the umbrella of trees, set against the darkening sky. Pinpricks of starlight dotted the heavens. The air had cooled to a warm, lulling breeze. One couldn't have asked for a more perfect night.

"You were right about your secret recipe. If you ever decide to get out of politics, you could bottle that stuff and make a mint." She wiped her mouth with the linen napkin and placed it down on the circular wooden table.

Preston's smile was triumphant. "Don't think I haven't considered it."

She glanced at him. "Do you think you would ever get out of politics?"

He inhaled deeply. "There were times in the early days of my career when I was in an office no bigger than a public bathroom, and I spent my time walking the streets, talking to the people, handing out flyers and palm cards and I would think that these problems are too big. What makes you think you can change things? And then there would be the one woman who didn't get kicked out of her apartment or the store that didn't have to close because I had helped in some way. Became the voice that they didn't have." He stared off toward the moon. "And then I'd realize that I could make a difference. Maybe not change the world, but change a life, many lives." He turned and looked into her eyes. "You know."

She nodded. "Yeah, I do."

"So I stuck with it and probably will for as long as the people will have me. While I was a councilman, it was local. Now as a senator I can help on a bigger scale. Hopefully do more good. Like with the Gulf and the education reform bill and pushing both Houses to get off their asses and rebuild the Ninth Ward in N'awlins." He tossed back the rest of his drink.

A flash of lightning streaked across the sky followed by the distant rumble of thunder.

Preston pushed up from his seat. "Better get these things inside before we get rained on," he said, glancing skyward.

They quickly gathered up their dishes and trays and covered the grill with a tarp but not before the heavens opened and got them pretty wet. They darted inside and slid the door closed behind them.

Their laughter and squishy footsteps played off each other all the way to the kitchen. "That was a surprise," Lee Ann said over her giggles. Water dripped down the side of her face.

Preston grabbed a paper towel from the rack and dabbed at her face. Then he ran his hands through her damp hair. The outline of her full breasts stood out against the fabric of her wet dress, teasing him, drawing his eyes to them. "Shouldn't last long." He wiped his face with the towel he'd used for Lee Ann, embedding her scent in his pores. He turned on the dishwasher then leaned against the counter and focused on Lee Ann. "We still have the rest of the evening…if you want," he said, reaching for her. She took his hand and came closer. "I'm hoping you want to stay for a while…the night…"

Lee Ann tried to swallow over the sudden dryness of her throat. Preston touched her cheek with the touch of his finger, and she felt as if she'd been shot with a bolt of that lightning that was illuminating the heavens. He gently cupped her cheek and stared deeply into her eyes.

"All day, every time I looked at you I couldn't stop myself from imagining making love to you."

The words like a caress stroked her, trembling her inner thighs.

"Will you stay with me tonight?"

She had no one to report to. Her siblings should be busy with their own exciting lives. Her father was in Washington. She was a grown woman, thoroughly attracted to this handsome, sexy man who wanted her. What was there to think about? But she had to think about it. This was not your everyday man; this was a U.S. senator, and whatever happened between them— good or bad—could easily become public knowledge. She was a private person. But…

He took one of her fingers in his mouth and gently sucked the tip. Her eyelids fluttered for an instant. He searched her face, waited for her answer. The heat of desire emanated off her in waves. He felt it, but he also felt her hesitancy. He drew her closer, and her heart pounded against his chest.

Lee Ann drew in a short breath. She ran her finger along his hairline then down around his jaw.

Preston took her hand and kissed the inside of her palm. Heat leaped up her arm. His tongue flicked across her wrist, and he watched the sensation shimmy down her body. He placed a hot kiss where his tongue had been.

His gaze danced to meet hers, and in its depths, Lee Ann saw her future waiting there for her to say, "Yes."

Relief mixed with a crazy new excitement, and a steady building need crawled through him. He lowered his head and took her welcoming mouth, savoring the sweet goodness of her lips, the texture of her tongue as it played with his, the feel of her lush curves that pressed teasingly against his body.

Lee Ann's fingers played at the base of his neck before trailing down the slope of his back to rest near the base of his spine. She splayed her fingers and stroked the broad, hard lines of him, up and down in an almost hypnotic motion.

Preston groaned. He moved closer, finding a temporary sanctuary for the hard length of his pulsing cock against the warmth of her soft stomach. He cupped her firm, round rear, and they both shuddered. He knew that if he kept that up he'd lose himself all over them both right there leaning up against the kitchen counter. Instead, he snaked his arm around her waist. She felt small and fragile, protected in the cocoon of his embrace. But he knew that Lee Ann Lawson may be a lot of things, but weak and vulnerable were not those things. She was strong and determined, sexy, smart, sweet and funny and the complexity of appearance and reality were such turn-ons that he couldn't think straight. The growing need to consume her and wrap her up in all that he was, share with her the strength and essence that was him, had him forgetting the real reason for this night of seduction. He pulled her closer, kissing her deeper, caressed her more urgently and pushed those other thoughts away and let himself become enmeshed in the magic web that she'd spun around him.

Lee Ann knew that this was probably too soon, too reckless even as she dipped her tongue deeper into his mouth. What was happening went against her good common sense and conservative nature, she thought as she wound her pelvis against him. But from the moment she met Preston it was as if a light had gone on inside that dim place in her soul. And she began to long for something more, something that was just for her. She didn't know if whatever this thing was that sparked between them would last forever, a few weeks, a month or no longer than tonight. It didn't matter. She wanted *it* and *him*.

Preston's hot lips drifted down the long line of her neck, found the tender sensitive spots and dropped heated kisses and searing flicks of his tongue until her tiny tremors began to slide up her throat and became aching sighs of desire.

He felt like a rogue in one of those romance novels when he swept her up into his arms and slowly carried her upstairs to his bedroom. She was light and so very womanly in his arms, and the look of desire that parted her lips, warmed her skin and sparked in her eyes had him on the brink of losing control. He knew he had to take his time and not succumb to the aching longing that held him in a vice grip.

Preston pushed open his bedroom door with his shoulder and carried her to his bed. Gently he lay her down on the thick mocha-colored comforter of his bed then sat beside her. He brushed away the hair that feathered her forehead and studied the face that stared back at him with anticipation, and suddenly it was absolutely important to him that this be right, for both of them, that it not be some casual thing, a slap in the face to her father just to soothe his own ego. Lee Ann didn't warrant that, and as he leaned down to kiss her slightly parted lips, he knew that with her he could never be less than what she deserved.

Her fingers gathered up the collar of his T-shirt and pulled him toward her. She wanted him. She wanted the full weight of Preston's hard body stretched out on hers, her legs entwined around his broad back. She wanted to feel the heft of his sex fill her wet walls and swell with his need of her. That's what she wanted—wanted so suddenly, so intensely that she could barely breathe.

She tugged at his shirt from the waist. "Take it off," she said in an urgent, harsh whisper.

Preston adjusted his position and dutifully did as he was told.

Her soft palms covered the outline of his chest as she

slowly rotated them over the rise of his nipples, which had hardened at her touch. Her tongue flicked over one then the other and back again, sending shockwaves of delight running along Preston's spine.

"You know," he whispered in her ear while they slowly gyrated against each other, "as a man of politics I firmly believe in quid pro quo."

A shadow of a smile moved along her mouth. Her gaze was hot and heavy. "I'd heard that about you Senate types." She ran her tongue along his bottom lip. "What did you have in mind, Senator Graham?"

His left hand snaked along her thigh and beneath the hem of her dress and pushed it up over her hips. She drew in a sharp breath when his hot palm captured the warm mound and caressed her through her damp panties. Lee Ann whimpered with delight and lifted her hips in response to the titillating sensations that rippled through her. His fingers teased along the thin elastic of the waistband. Lee Ann lifted up and Preston pulled her black lace panties down over her hips, and she wiggled out of them, kicking them to the floor.

Preston stared at what awaited him between butter-soft skin and tight thighs nestled in a bed of silky, short black hair. Turned on by the sight of her quivering inner thighs when he ran his fingers up and down them, he gently pushed her legs wider apart and bent her knees. Lee Ann gasped with pleasure while his thumb trailed across her clit that peeked out through the folds and began to swell. He did it again and again and again until she was slick and wet and trembling, gripping the sheets in her fists as if they could keep her from falling under his erotic spell.

Her body jerked as he slid one finger inside of her. Hot liquid flowed over his fingertip, making it easy for two to enter, move in and out of her, preparing her for what was to come, making her want it as much as he did.

"Ohhh…right there, right there," she groaned. "Oh, ohhh, aggg. Preston…" She cupped her hand over his when his long middle finger found her spot. Her legs opened wider. Her hips rose and fell in time to the rhythmic in and out. She guided the pressure, kept his finger gently massaging her goldmine, a hidden treasure that she'd heard about, read about but had never found or experienced until now. The feeling was so intense that every fiber of her being seemed to be on fire. She saw stars behind her closed lids, her thoughts rocked back and forth—yes, no, yes—her body was no longer her own but one consumed by desire, and at the same time she wanted to deny it and allow this maddening pleasure to go on forever.

Preston could feel the build of her orgasm in the sporadic tightening and release of her inner walls around his fingers. Her entire body tightened then popped as if struck by a jolt of electricity. He was torn between bringing her to climax or experiencing it together with him buried deep within the sweet wetness that was begging him to come hither.

As if reading his mind, Lee Ann whispered, "I want this with you inside me."

Preston massaged the spot again. Her body arched in response. She cried out. "Are you sure?" He did it again.

"Yes, yes." The hand that had guided his now grabbed

his wrist and held it with a strength that surprised him. "Now."

Preston stood up, unbuckled then unzipped his shorts, stepped out of his briefs and pushed them aside with his foot.

Air shuddered in her chest when she looked at him. His erection was full, long, thick and throbbing.

Preston extended his hand to her. She placed her hand in his, and he pulled her to her feet. He turned her around and began to unzip her dress, placing hot kisses on her back across each inch that was revealed until he'd reached the end, peeling her dress down as he went until he was on his knees. Grabbing her hips, he turned her back around, and the heat of her sex met his waiting tongue. He licked. She swayed against him. He held the perfect globes of her ass in his hands, kneading them while urging her forward.

She couldn't think. Her body was totally in control. She needed a minute to breathe, but she couldn't. He was doing crazy things to her, new things that were driving her wild in a way she'd never experienced. She was scared. His tongue played with her clit, back and forth, gently sucked it. She screamed and dug her fingers into his shoulders. He licked. She weakened.

Preston eased her back toward the bed until her knees bumped the mattress. He pressed his hand between the swell of her breasts and eased her down onto her back while draping her legs over his shoulders, leaving her wide open and vulnerable to everything within the arsenal of his imagination. He intended to drive her to the brink of sexual sanity and take her over the edge.

Tremors fluttered across her belly. His tongue dipped

inside of her, seeking her spot. He teased and probed, suckled and laved.

"Press...pleassse..."

"Please, what baby..." he said between succulent mouthfuls of her.

Her body shook with sobs of ecstasy. "I...I can't...I want...awwwww." She rocked her hips against him, tried to get up but couldn't.

Preston tightened his hold on her thighs. She wasn't getting away, not yet. "Come on, baby. Let it go," he coaxed, intensifying his sensual pursuit of her. He suckled the swollen, thrumming clit until her entire body stiffened, air was sucked into her lungs and held there, and then the cascade of release that began at the balls of her feet loosened and tightened the muscles of her legs, jettisoned up her spine, flooded her extremities before returning with full force to the epicenter of her womanhood, opening and closing in powerful bursts. She released her cries as she thrashed on the bed, her mind and body splitting before crashing back together to leave her limp and trembling.

Preston scooped her up and laid her on the bed with her head resting on the thick pillows. Her lashes fluttered, and her eyes slowly focused on him as he lowered himself above her, leveraging his weight on his arms.

Her body hummed. Her thoughts were still cloudy as she felt the steady pressure of his shaft push against her pulsing opening. She spread her thighs in longing.

Preston dipped his head and found her taut nipple and drew it into his mouth, sucking it like ripe fruit that sent waves of pleasure shooting to her stomach. He raised up on his knees and cupped her to him. "Look at me," he commanded in a hard and ragged voice, and in a long, single thrust he broke past her slickened opening. His strangled cry of delight merged with hers and filled the room.

That instant of connection was terrifying in its power. It consumed them, altered them in a way that they couldn't understand. The sensation was beyond words as they found their special rhythm and rode on a tide of bliss that rose and fell and rose again, carrying them off to a place that neither had ever experienced before.

Lee Ann clung to him, her arms and legs wrapped around his body as his thrusts grew harder, deeper, faster and more demanding and urgent until she knew he would split her in two, yet she didn't want it to end. It was too good, too delicious.

Preston's deep groans grew in intensity, and he knew he couldn't hold back much longer, not with her walls singing the sweetest song, gripping him, stroking him. He shuddered from head to toe. His jaw clenched as the first spasm jerked his scrotum, stiffened his cock and shot through it again and again, sending a flood of his essence into her waiting body.

The feeling of his release set off Lee Ann's climax, which lifted her hips off the bed and spread her legs so wide and so high that Preston found heaven.

Their rapid breathing and soft sighs floated around them as their bodies unwound and they slowly returned to earth.

Tenderly Preston kissed her swollen lips, wiped the dampness from her forehead. He had no words. There were none to explain what had happened between them. Reluctantly, he rolled off her then cradled her against him, trying to get his mind right.

Lee Ann listened to the steady beat of his heart, which matched her own. She closed her eyes and savored this moment, this perfect afterglow. No man had ever done to her what Preston had done. Ever. She'd never felt like that before, been made love to like that before. Was he like this with other women? Had he made others feel what he made her feel? No, she couldn't let her mind take her there. This was her time. And come what may that could never be taken from her.

Sometime during the night, Preston had put her under the sheet, she realized—half awake and half asleep. She felt his warm breath brush against her neck and the pressure of his leg that was draped across hers and his arm that secured her around the waist. She sighed in contentment and snuggled back to sleep.

Chapter 6

Lee Ann was awakened by the scent of fresh brewing coffee. She blinked against the haze of the early morning light and peered at the bedside clock—6:30 a.m. She jumped up and looked around. This wasn't her bedroom. She was naked and sticky and aching all over. She squeezed her eyes shut. She'd never made it home last night. Inwardly she groaned, dreading the third degree that she was sure to get when she walked in the door. She flopped back down on the bed and then thought better of it and went in search of her clothes, just as Preston walked in the door with a mug of coffee in his hands.

"Now that's what I call a beautiful sight in the morning—a naked woman in a man's bed." He crossed the room.

Lee Ann bent over and recovered her underwear.

"Morning," she muttered. She snatched the sheet from the bed and halfway wrapped it around her.

"I've seen it all, sweet," he said coming up to her and tugging the sheet away. His eyes raked over her then settled on her face. He lifted her chin with the tip of his finger. "How are you this morning?"

"I don't know yet." She didn't meet his gaze.

"Here, have some of this." He gave her the coffee with one hand and fondled her exposed breasts with the other. "You were incredible," he said, the awesomeness of it still new to him.

She trembled beneath his touch and tried to concentrate on not rattling the mug and emptying the hot contents all over the both of them.

"I was going for my morning jog, but I didn't want you to wake up and not find me here."

"I probably should be getting home."

He clasped her shoulders and gazed down into her eyes. "Relax. Take a shower. Read the paper. When I get back, we can have some breakfast and I'll drive you home."

She'd never hear the end of it if they saw her pulling up to the house in Preston's car after having been out all night—something that she had never done.

"No. You don't have to do that."

"I want to." He frowned. "What is it?"

"Nothing." She turned away from him and set the mug on the nightstand. "I'm going to take a shower."

He held up his hands and backed off. "Fine. The bathroom is the first door on the right. There are towels and whatever else you need on the shelf in there."

"Thank you," she muttered. With as much dignity

as she could summon, she walked her very naked self out of the bedroom.

Lee Ann shut the bathroom door behind her, looked around and found the closed cabinet that held the towels. She opened the shower stall and turned on the water, then flipped down the toilet seat top and sat down. She covered her face with her hands. What a mess. As much as she enjoyed, thrilled in her night with Preston, she should have been thinking with her head and not her starved libido. They hadn't used protection. She'd spent the night with him. Her family had probably been calling all night. She moaned. What was she going to tell them? And what if…

Preston returned from his run, and he could tell the moment that he walked through the door that Lee Ann was gone. There was a new kind of silence in the house, even as Rocky came to greet him.

He trotted up the steps to his bedroom hoping that she was still there even though he knew that she wasn't. He pushed open the door. The bed was made. The used sheets were stuffed in a pillowcase and sat by the side of the bed. There was nothing left of her. It was as if she'd never been there, and he didn't understand why she seemed to want it that way.

He tossed his keys on the dresser and pulled his damp shirt over his head and flipped it onto the pile of sheets. This had all gone wrong. He drew in a long, deep breath wanting to catch a hint of her scent. His plan had been to seduce her, to rub her father's nose in it and show him that Preston Graham was not someone he could push around, threaten.

He crossed the room and walked to the window that looked out onto his front lawn. It was he who'd been seduced, whose brain had been put on scramble. The question now was what was he going to do about it.

Lee Ann quietly closed the door behind her. She looked up the staircase then across both sides of the wide hallway. She started for the stairs and hoped that she could at least get to her room before she ran into anyone.

On the ride over in the cab, she'd checked her cell phone. Her father had called three times. He was demanding as usual at first, annoyed the second time and by his third call he was bordering on furious and worried. Dominique and Desiree had texted her all night, and there were even two from Justin, all wanting to know where she was. The one and only text that brought a bit of smile to her face was the one from Rafe. "Hey sis, don't let the fam hassle u. Njoy ur nite. U deserve it. R"

She drew in a breath as she rounded the top of the landing and walked down the hallway to her room. She opened her door and gasped in alarm.

Dominique and Desiree were both curled on her bed. She shut her eyes for a moment and closed the door behind her. Dominique stirred, rubbed her eyes. Slowly she sat up and nudged Desiree. Desiree grumbled. She was nudged again. "Get up. She's here."

Desiree struggled to sit up. She pushed her wild curls out of her face. "Daddy was freaking," she said, her voice croaking.

Dominique adjusted her head scarf that had slid down

her forehead. "Forty-eight hours. I told you about 48 hours," Dominique complained. "Daddy was a minute away from calling the police."

Lee Ann huffed. "This is ridiculous. I'm thirty-three years old. If I want to stay out until Santa comes down the chimney I can stay out! Why does the whole world need to know about every move that I make?" She stomped across the room and threw her purse onto the side chair then kicked off her sandals.

Her sisters watched her in openmouthed astonishment. Who was this woman?

Lee Ann snatched up her hairbrush, and they both ducked. She ran it roughly across her short hair, pulling her hair flat and smooth across her head. Her sharp features and hazel eyes appeared to be lit up from underneath.

"Now please leave, and if I feel like telling either of you anything I'll let you know."

They popped up from the bed and skulked to the door, not daring to say a word, their usual bantering absent.

Lee Ann swung the door shut behind them. She spun away, vacillating between outrage and embarrassment. Today she should be joyous, reveling in an extraordinary night with an incredible man. Instead, she was angry, scared and humiliated. She pushed her purse out of the way and plopped down in the chair. What was she going to do now?

The muffled sound of her phone floated up to her from her purse. She reached for it and dug out her phone. The number was Preston's.

She squeezed the phone in her hand, hesitated and

then finally pressed Talk before the call could go to voice mail.

"Hello?"

"I wanted to make sure you got home safely. I would have taken you."

"I'm fine. Really."

An awkward silence hung between them.

"Lee Ann…I'm not sure what's going on in your head, what went wrong or even if something did." He'd never felt so inadequate in his life. He was a man who stood in front of hundreds of people and convinced them to believe in his ability to make things right. Yet, here he was fumbling around like a kid caught sneaking in after curfew and not knowing how to explain.

She sighed. "Preston, I have a really full day ahead of me. I'm fine. I'll call you. Okay?"

That was his line! "Sure. Fine. Have a good day." He disconnected the call and wondered why he'd bothered.

Lee Ann's eyes stung. She pushed herself up from her seat, went to her closet to find a change of clothes and steel her mind for her call to her father. It was a call she wanted to put off for as long as possible.

Preston slammed the ball against the wall with his racquet, and it sounded like a gunshot in the enclosed court.

"Okay, okay I give up." Paul Dubois huffed, sweat streaming down his face. "You're playing like a madman."

Paul bent in half to catch his breath. Preston's sneakers screeched against the floor as he came to a stop. He snatched up the ball and slid down the wall and rested on his haunches.

"You wanna tell me what's buggin' you?" Paul wiped his face with a towel and squatted down next to Preston.

Preston leaned his head back against the wall and dropped the towel over his face.

"Must be a woman," Paul said, scrubbing his face with his towel and rotating his wrist.

Paul was the only friend who Preston could honestly say was a friend. They'd grown up together, Preston in the home of a poor single mother, and Paul with a middle-class mom and dad, picket fence and a dog. Their friendship was as much an accident as one could have—literally. Preston ran Paul down with his bike while he was trying to get away from the fruit vendor with the bag of fruit he'd stolen. Luc, the vendor, collared them both and threatened to call the police. Paul pulled money out of his pocket and paid for the fruit. "That should cover it," he'd said in that often dismissive way of his that was present even at the age of twelve. Preston could almost hear Paul saying, "Now be gone with you," like some British royal, even though France ran through his blood.

"Is it?" Paul asked.

"Something like that."

"Hmm, that clears up everything." He rested his head on his knees.

Preston pushed up from the floor and began to pace, cuing Paul that his best friend was in contemplation mode. When he stopped walking, he'd hesitate a beat and spew it all out in a rush. Paul waited, and like perfect choreography that had been honed by years of repetition, Preston told him about Lee Ann Lawson.

"Senator Lawson's daughter?" Paul shook his head. "You sure can pick 'em."

"Thanks, Paul."

"You barely know her. How did you get yourself all twisted up?"

"It's…it's not something that I can explain," he said, and the reality of saying the words out loud only solidified Lee Ann's inexplicable impact on him. "When I first met her I was like, 'Wow,' totally blown away, and it freaked me out. And then when her father pretty much told me to leave her alone and concentrate on my career that just pissed me off. Who the hell does he think he is?"

"Uh, one of the most powerful senators in the United States."

Preston threw him a look. Paul shrugged.

"So you slept with her to stick it to her father—no pun intended—and now you're left with the morning-after blues."

Preston snorted and started pacing again. He stopped and turned to Paul. "I ran into Charlotte the other night, and she started leaving messages on my house phone."

"Now that is a problem—for you. Told you to change your number a long time ago. Charlotte is only going to mess up your head again."

"She asked to see me."

Now Paul got up, stood toe to toe with Preston. "Don't even think about it, man."

"She's engaged."

"So what. She was engaged to you, too. It means nothing to her. She's poison."

"I agreed to meet her."

Paul slapped his forehead. "What!"

"She called right after I talked to Lee Ann this morning. I was pissed and…"

"And your ego decided to be in charge since you obviously weren't thinking clearly enough with your little head. Hey—" he threw up his hands "—it's not a problem. Don't show up. Simple."

Preston looked away.

"You're not thinking of going."

"Just drinks."

"Right. Nothing with Charlotte is *just* anything. She is Ms. Agenda. And you're it." He shook his head in disgust and frustration. He ran his hand across his inky waves. "What about Lee Ann? I mean it might be kind of rough with Papa Lawson…but it sounds like you could really care about her…that you *do* care about her."

Preston's jaw clenched. "She said what she had to say."

"Did it occur to you that she wanted *you* to say something?"

"I did. I asked her if she got home all right."

"You know what your problem is?"

"I'm sure you're going to tell me."

Paul pointed a finger at him. "You are so used to sex with no commitment after the fiasco with Charlotte that you don't know how to handle a potentially good thing when it's sitting on your bed."

Preston frowned. "I gotta go."

Paul knew Preston sometimes better than he knew himself. His pat "gotta go" line was a signal that he didn't have the answer to a very legitimate question. In other words, Preston was done talking. He picked up his racquet and wrapped his towel around his neck. They walked out together. "When are you heading back up to the capital?"

"In the morning."

"I'll be up there when the voting begins—with the film crew. I hope you'll provide a few sound bites, Senator," he joked.

"I'll think about it. Let me know when you get into town."

"Sure."

They walked into the showers.

Standing under the beating water, Preston thought about Paul's warning while he lathered. Yeah, Charlotte was trouble. She'd ripped him apart, and for a long time, he never thought he would recover. He'd grown bitter and distant. Commitment was out of the question for him. So he'd channeled all of his energies—good and bad—into building his career, into winning. And with time, the anger began to fade and the wound wasn't quite as deep, and he could look at women again as more than sexual objects. He'd started to get his humanity back. Meeting Lee Ann and feeling that old stir again was exciting and scary. There was still that part of him that didn't trust his feelings, didn't trust women. Yet, Lee Ann seemed different, and from the moment they met, he couldn't stop thinking about her, wanting her. Then last night…a shiver of desire ran through him and his penis jerked in response.

He heard the water go off in the stall next to him. Moments later, Paul called out, "I have a meeting at the studio. Gotta run. I'll catch up with you later."

"Yeah. Later." Preston took his time finishing up his shower and then decided to spend twenty minutes in the steam room to get out the last kinks of tension.

When he emerged from the sports club he did feel better, clearheaded and back in control of his body. He strode across the parking lot to his SUV, deactivated the alarm and was about to step inside when his cell phone rang. It was a call that was being forwarded from his home phone, one of the few features he used but came in handy when he was away from home for long periods of time. He'd just reset it that morning.

"Hello?"

"Is this a bad time?"

The voice lifted the fine hairs on the back of his neck. "A bad time for what, Charlotte?"

"To meet. I've been making myself crazy thinking about seeing you later. I was hoping that you were free."

Typical Charlotte. At the drop of a dime, she wanted what she wanted. All of Paul's warnings rang in his head, that Sunday afternoon years earlier, the diamond that sparkled on her finger, Lee Ann…. "Listen, about later, it's not cool. I can't meet you."

"What, but you said—"

"I don't want to see you, Charlotte. It was a mistake even talking to you."

"I know why you don't want to see me," she said in a rush, "because you still have feelings for me, just like I do for you. You remember how it was between us. The passion that we had for each other. I know you remember, but you think I'm going to hurt you again. I swear to you, I won't. Just give me another chance, Press, please."

"I gotta go." He disconnected the call even as he heard her say his name. He glanced around for a moment, looked down at the phone, almost expecting it to ring again. Finally, he got up in his ride and drove off.

"Thanks for meeting me, Rafe," Lee Ann said as they found seats in the back of the Pompei Bistro.

"Anything for you." He set down his tray, took a napkin and dabbed at his forehead. He glanced at his sister from beneath his sweeping dark lashes. Their crazy family had her in knots. The tight line between her eyes would need a chisel to carve it away. "Talk to Daddy?" He picked up half of his shrimp po'boy sandwich and took a big juicy bite. He knew that she must have; if not Branford Lawson would have been on the first plane back from DC.

"He talked to me is more like it."

"Hmm, know what that's like."

She pushed her salad around on her plate then looked across at her brother and oddly her best friend. As much as he was known for his wild and carefree ways, Rafe was caring and sensitive, and he understood her and he had good common sense, especially about life and relationships—his specialty. But most of all, she could trust him to listen and not judge her, whether he agreed with her or not.

"I wasn't thinking," she finally said.

Rafe chewed and waited.

"He's just so… He makes me feel things. Things I'd forgotten about." She put her fork down and looked at him. "Do you know what I mean?"

"Absolutely. Happens to me all the time."

"Be serious!"

"I am." He put his sandwich down and wiped his mouth. He leaned forward. "Look, ever since Mama died, you've stepped into her shoes. All you do is work and take care of the family. We…kind of expect that from you. But the truth is we're all grown, Lee, and as long as you feel like no one can handle anything but you…well, we let you handle it. And that goes for the old man, too." He reached for his iced tea and wished he had a shot of bourbon to splash in it. "So how do you feel about this guy?"

"I like him…a lot."

He watched the rainbow of expressions that moved across her face. "So what are you gonna do about it?"

She played with her food some more. "I guess I should call him. He must think I'm crazy for acting the way I did. Running out of there like my panties were on fire."

"They probably were."

She tossed her napkin at him, which he snatched in midair. "Very funny." She stared at her plate then focused on her brother, who was making quick work of his sandwich.

Rafe chuckled and chewed. "Men are used to women acting crazy. That's half the fun."

She studied her food for a minute, debating on how to phrase what she wanted to say. "I know you're a very busy man with the ladies and I was wondering if you could tell me the best place to get some flavored condoms," she blurted out in a hot whisper. "And maybe some ribbed ones."

Rafe choked, reached for his glass of iced tea and took a long swallow, gagging in the process. Coughing and wiping his eyes, he got himself together and looked at Lee Ann through watery eyes. "Are you kidding me?" He looked around. "Am I being punked?"

She stared right at him. "Nope." It took all she had not to burst out laughing. In all her years, it was truly the rare occasion that her big brother got flustered.

"Lee Ann...you're my sister for chrissake." If he could have turned red he would have.

"Yes, and you're my best friend and a man. You know what men like or what you like. If I can't ask you…"

He blew out a long breath and signaled for the waitress. "Can we have the check, please?"

"What are you doing?"

"Come on," he said, throwing money on the table.

"Where are we going?"

He took her by the hand and tugged her out of her seat. "Let's go. You want to get all up in my sex life." He looked down at her and winked. "I'll take you to one of my special places."

She snatched up her purse and stumbled out behind him.

Nearly two hours later they were sitting in his car. Lee Ann had a discrete little brown shopping bag, filled with an assortment of condoms in every flavor of the rainbow, along with massage oils, edible undies and dusting powder.

"How do you know about…that store?" she asked, looking into her bag of goodies.

"Stumbled on it a few years ago. From the outside you would never know. It's real classy."

She nodded and looked at him with a grin.

He started up the engine.

"Rafe…"

"Yeah?"

"Thanks."

He turned to her and patted her thigh. "Give the man a call. Tell the crew to mind their own business. Daddy, too. They aren't gonna like it, but they'll get over it. Live your life, cher. Do that for me? Mama would have wanted you to."

Her throat tightened. She wished that her mother was still there, that she could rest her head on her lap and tell her all the things that were going on in her head and in her heart. She swallowed and willed herself not to cry.

"But I'm telling you. If he hurts you, he's gonna have me to deal with." He hit the gas and pulled off.

Lee Ann glanced at her brother and never loved him more.

Preston opened the door to his house after taking Rocky for his evening walk. He'd come through that door hundreds of times but never had it felt so empty inside.

He hung up Rocky's leash and went to turn on the news. He had a 9:00 a.m. flight and he needed to pack, but what he wanted to do was call Lee Ann and find out what the hell went wrong. He stretched out on the couch. Women.

Rachel Maddow was interviewing the embattled president of the RNC. Preston tried to concentrate but his thoughts kept wandering back to his night with Lee Ann. Tomorrow he would see her father, and he wasn't up for any kind of confrontation. But it seemed like Senator Lawson always got his wish anyway. That fact alone punched up his ticked-off meter. He aimed the remote at the television and shut it off, threw his legs over the side and pushed up.

Being a first-term senator, he didn't have one of the fancier apartments in the nation's capital but it was functional and comfortable. He'd enjoyed being in DC at the heart of the nation in the months that he'd been in office. This time he was returning with a different kind of agenda—work until he worked Lee Ann out of his head.

He opened his bedroom door, and he could almost see her curled beneath the sheets.

"Damn it." He kicked at the door, slamming it against the wall. He stalked over to his closet and pulled out his traveling bag, went to his dresser, pulled open drawers and started tossing things in the bag, not caring what was winding up in the growing pile. He took his shaving kit from the dresser drawer and tossed it in the bag where it landed softly on a mound of T-shirts and at least two dozen pairs of socks. What was he doing? He had suits and shirts at his DC apartment and workout clothes, shoes and underwear. He looked at the haphazard contents of his bag and groaned at his own stupidity.

He blew out a breath of frustration and began picking through the items when Rocky started barking at the ringing doorbell. He checked his watch. It must be his house sitter, Merna, who'd come for the keys. He grabbed the extra set from the top of the dresser and trotted downstairs. He pulled open the door.

"Hi."

"What are you doing here?"

Chapter 7

"You coming in?" Lee Ann asked when they came to a stop on the driveway of the Lawson mansion.

"Not tonight, cher. I have a lovely lady waiting for the pleasure of my company."

Lee Ann shook her head and giggled. "You are a hot mess."

"So they tell me." He leaned over and kissed her cheek. "I'll call you."

She opened her door and then looked at him over her shoulder. "Thanks again."

"You just do like I said—live your life. And give that man a call."

She nodded. "I will." She shut the door, and he backed out.

"What you need is your own place," he called out from the window before he roared away.

Lee Ann walked up the steps to the home she'd

lived in since she was born. The history of the Lawson home was long and rich, filled with old wives' tales and folklore. Like many of the big homes in Louisiana, this was once a plantation, the grounds dotted with slaves; the small houses in the back of the property that were now used for storage were once slave cabins. After the Emancipation, the slaves of the house didn't leave the only land that they knew. The owner, Hezikiah Lawson, who'd fallen in love with Mary, one of his slaves, turned over his land and all of his money to her and their children upon his death. Mary had a long and hard struggle fighting the law and the other landowners to hold on to her property and her children's rightful inheritance, but she did. Rumor had it that she sat on the porch every night with a shotgun across her lap and would shoot anyone who tried to step onto her property. The freed slaves admired and respected Mary and continued to work the land, making Mary and her family very wealthy. From 1872 until now the house had been handed down generation after generation. At least that's how the story was told.

Lee Ann turned the knob and opened the door. She looked around at the exquisite interior, the space that guests always oohed and aahed over but which she thought of as the hallway. The marble floors were where she'd roller-skated with Rafe, and they were always sent to sit in the kitchen with the cook as punishment. Dom and Desi would slide down the winding banister every morning as their father bellowed for them to stop.

Inwardly she smiled. This was home. She'd never thought much about living anyplace else. When Rafe moved out and bought a small house on the other side of town, you would have thought that it was the apocalypse the way their father carried on. Every chance he got, he reminded Rafe how he was breaking up the family. It was only after much soothing and gentle but firm admonishment from her mother that Branford finally relented, albeit reluctantly. Louisa, her mother, was the only one who could get through to her father once he got something in his head. Now that responsibility had fallen on her shoulders.

Lee Ann sighed and started up the stairs. Rafe still kept his room here at the house—almost as a peace offering—but he'd wanted his freedom, and Rafe was not the type to be denied what he wanted.

Lee Ann opened her bedroom door, walked over to the window and pulled back the curtains. *A place of her own.* It wasn't something she'd thought much about, but after last night's fiasco with her family and Rafe putting the "flee the coop" bug in her ear... She let the curtain fall back in place.

What would it be like to bring Preston to her place? She took off her shoes and put them inside the closet, unbuttoned her top and slipped it off.

The downstairs door slammed shut, and the chattering of her sisters floated upstairs, coming closer. She took a lightweight robe from the closet and put it on then stepped out of her skirt. With any luck they would take the hint and walk past her closed door.

The voices came to a stop in front of her door. Lee Ann waited. And then a white envelope was slipped under the door, like something out of a spy movie. She went over and picked up the envelope, flipped it over and opened it. She took out the single piece of handwritten paper.

Dear Sis,
We're really sorry. Don't be mad. We were worried. It was weird not having you here and kind of scary. So whenever you forgive us we want to hear all about him!
Love
D & D

Lee Ann refolded the letter and put it back in the envelope. She pressed it to her chest and smiled, placing it on the top of her dresser. Any other time she would have been wallowing in guilt and looking for ways to make it up to everyone, soothe their ruffled feathers. She raised her chin just a bit higher. She had a call to make. Let them sweat it out a little longer.

"I asked you what you were doing here, Charlotte."

"You wouldn't come to me. You left me no choice." She sucked on her glossy bottom lip. "Are we going to stand here and discuss our business for your neighbors, or are you going to let me in?"

"We don't have any business."

"I think we do."

"Goodbye, Charlotte." He tried to push the door closed.

"What if I told you I could make sure you got the funding you needed to rebuild your district and get the money for schools?"

His brow wrinkled. "What are you talking about?"

She watched him hesitate. "You'd be the golden boy," she said, pressing home her point. "You'd be able to pull off what the old dogs haven't been able to do in years."

He stared at her for a long moment. Even contemplating having Charlotte involved in his life—his political life was less than practical. But if there was one thing he knew about Charlotte Dupree, it was that when it came to behind-the-scenes dealings she always came out on top. She was a woman who knew what pie to keep her hand in.

"At least listen to what I have to say."

Against his better judgment, he stepped aside and let her in.

Charlotte strolled in, looked around in that surveying way of hers as if every room that she walked into could potentially become her property. "Things haven't changed much," she said, dropping her purse on the couch. "The picture on the wall is new." She turned to him, her magazine cover smile in place.

"You wanted to talk, and I'm sure it's not about my taste in art. So talk." He took a seat farthest away from her.

She pretended to pout. "You used to be such a gentleman. Can't you even offer me something to drink? Or should I get it myself."

"I'm sure you remember where everything is."

She tsk-tsked and crossed the small space to the side bar. "Bourbon, right?" She bent over and pulled open the cabinet.

Preston averted his gaze. "Yeah."

She poured them both a drink and came to stand in

front of him. The hem of her short skirt met him at eye level. "Cheers," she said, handing him his drink.

He didn't respond.

Charlotte shook her shoulders and sauntered back to her seat. She sat down and crossed her long legs in slow motion, hiking her short dress up her firm thighs. For an instant, Preston wondered if she still wore the tiny silver clit ring. When they made love, it would drive her wild and him wilder. He glanced away and took a long swallow of his bourbon, letting the amber liquid burn away the image.

"Your fiancé know you're here?" he asked, feeling suddenly nasty and edgy.

"I go where I want. Anthony doesn't question me." She sipped her drink and studied him.

"You want to get to the point of your visit?"

"I thought we could chat first, catch up."

Preston sprung up from his seat and was right up on her before she could blink. He plucked the glass from her hand. "Goodbye, Charlotte." He took her arm. "I don't have time for your games. Come on. Let's go."

"All right, all right. Take it easy." She shrugged to get her arm out of his grasp. "Tony is a lobbyist."

Preston frowned.

"He represents the oil companies."

He let go of her arm. "What are you saying?"

"He's looking for a team player. Someone to advocate for them against all of the new regulations that they could be facing. They're willing to make it worth your while."

Preston backed off, shaking his head.

"Just hear him out. What they are proposing could

benefit thousands of businesses and families on the Gulf. But they need to get more Democrats on board."

Preston held up his hand. "You're asking me to get in bed with the very people who caused this catastrophe in the first place? You're kidding right? This is some kind of hidden camera joke," he said, his disbelief boiling to outrage.

Charlotte stood. She looked straight at him. "I think you know that when it comes to business I don't joke around. I came to you because I know what this can do for your career—*long term*. It has the potential to take you all the way," she said with meaning, her brow lifting to punctuate her point. "You can be the one whose name is remembered in restoring this part of the Gulf. The people will remember when the time comes," she continued in an almost hypnotic cadence. She reached for her purse and took out a business card and handed it to him.

It was Anthony Paulsen's card with his private cell phone number. Preston almost did a double take. He thought the man he'd seen her with was vaguely familiar, but he didn't give it much thought. Charlotte was engaged to one of the most powerful lobbyists on Capitol Hill—without equal. He was young, talented and had the ear of all the right people.

"You're engaged to Anthony Paulsen?"

She shrugged offhandedly. "At least think about it."

"Is that a yes?"

"Yes. Okay. Happy now."

"Why are you doing this? Why do you even give a damn? There must be something in this for you."

She almost looked hurt. "I owe you," she said simply.

Preston exhaled heavily. He looked at the card. "I'm not promising anything."

His cell phone rang in his pocket. He pulled it out, and his pulse leaped. Lee Ann's number was illuminated on the screen. "Excuse me." He turned his back to Charlotte and walked to the other side of the room before he answered.

Charlotte knew that move all too well. Her green eyes narrowed. She could barely hear his muffled conversation, which only confirmed her suspicions. If this had been any other time when he'd finished with his call he'd turn around and find her naked, spread out on his couch and waiting. She closed her purse. There would be plenty of time for that.

"Hey. I wasn't sure if I was going to hear from you."

"I'm sorry about this morning. I don't know...I wasn't thinking or maybe I was thinking too much."

"No problem." He cleared his throat and waited. This time he was going to let her take the lead.

"What time is your flight?"

"Nine."

"Oh. Um...all packed?"

He thought about the mess upstairs. "Not exactly."

"Well, I should let you go. I just wanted to say I'm sorry...and that last night was incredible."

Preston felt as if a boulder had been lifted off his chest. "Yeah, it was."

She giggled.

"Listen, I know it's short notice, but if you felt like

coming by here tonight, we could ride to the airport together. I have a car picking me up at seven. The driver could bring you back home or drop you off wherever you needed to be."

The offer was more than tempting. She wanted to see him and make sure that everything she felt and had experienced wasn't some fluke. But she also considered the drama that her last foray had wrought.

"Say yes," he gently urged. "I'll come and get you."

"I need some time."

"Is an hour enough?"

"Yes." She moved around the room looking for what she'd need to take with her. "I have an eleven o'clock class tomorrow. I hope you won't mind if I bring some work with me."

"Bring whatever you want."

"How about if I drive you to the airport tomorrow?"

"You sure?"

"Yes, it'll be easier all the way around. I'll drive my car to you tonight and drop you off in the morning. Then I can go straight to the university and not have to worry about transportation."

"If you're sure."

"I am." She paused. "Are you?"

"I'll see you when you get here."

"Bye," she whispered and disconnected the call.

He palmed the phone and turned with the smile still on his face. He'd totally forgotten about Charlotte.

She was looking into the mirror of her compact and

fixing her lipstick. "She must be important." She pressed her lips together and snapped the compact shut.

"She is."

Charlotte started for the door. "Who is she?"

"None of your business."

She snickered. "Have it your way." She opened the door then turned to Preston. "It was good seeing you. Almost like old times." She reached out and brushed her thumb along his bottom lip. He grabbed her wrist. She laughed. "Think about the offer. Tony will be in DC at the end of the week. So will I." She walked out.

Lee Ann finished putting her things together in a small overnight tote, got her notes for class and put them in her computer bag. She opened her flowered makeup case and dropped in a handful of condoms. Her heart thumped. She placed her two bags near her bedroom door, took a last look around then went downstairs in search of her sisters.

She heard voices coming from the kitchen and peeked in. Justin was sitting at the table with Melba, the housekeeper and cook.

"Hi." She buzzed Justin's cheek and gave Melba a light squeeze.

"Hey, sis." Justin took a large bite of his apple. "What's up?"

"Dom and Desi around?"

"I saw Dominique go out back," Melba said. "I haven't seen Desiree."

"Thanks." She grabbed an apple from the bowl and walked through the kitchen to the enclosed sun porch and pushed open the sliding glass doors.

Dominique and Desiree were taking laps in the pool. Desiree spotted Lee Ann first and signaled her sister. They stroked to the edge and hoisted themselves up onto the deck.

Lee Ann held a towel in each hand.

"Thanks," they muttered and lightly dried off.

"I got your note." She looked from one sheepish face to the other. "I apologize for not calling anyone. That was wrong. But me having a life of my own isn't."

"Do you like him?" Desiree asked softly.

"That's what I'm trying to find out. And there will be times that I'm not going to be here—while I figure it out," she added with a soft smile. "But I promise to give you guys a heads-up. Okay? Like now."

The twins' identical looks of surprise were almost comical.

"I'll see you all tomorrow evening." She kissed each of their cheeks and turned to leave.

"Have fun," Desiree called out.

"Do something I would do," Dominique said.

Lee Ann shook her head in amusement as she slid the door closed behind her.

Preston finished putting away all of the things he didn't need and put what he did back in a black carryall. He set it by his dresser, checked his bedroom one last time then jogged downstairs just as he heard a car pulling into the driveway.

He crossed the hall and glanced into the front room. Two glasses sat on the coffee table. One with a clear red imprint of Charlotte's lips. He snatched them up and took them into the kitchen. Even as he stuck them in the dishwasher he wondered why he felt the need to hide them from Lee Ann.

The bell rang. He pressed Start and went to answer the door.

Where Charlotte's presence was like a storm brewing, Lee Ann was sunshine and rainbows, the prize after the fury.

"Hey," he greeted.

Her eyes flitted from his face to his chest and back again. "Hi." She shifted her bag on her shoulder.

"Here, let me take something."

She handed him her computer bag. Preston put his arm around her waist and closed the door behind them.

"You can use the office next to the kitchen if you want to work."

"Where will you be?" She set her bag down near his bedroom window, linked and unlinked her fingers then ran her hands along her denim-covered thighs.

Preston came to where she stood, close enough to see the flecks of gold in her eyes and feel the warmth of her body wrap around him. "Wherever you want me to be."

Lee Ann's stomach fluttered. She sunk into the depths of his eyes and lost herself.

Preston leaned down and kissed her so tenderly that she could have imagined it was a fantasy if it was not for the heat she felt on her lips.

"Hmm. You are real." His fingers threaded through her short hair, eased her closer. "You won't get any work done if we keep standing here much longer."

She ran her tongue across her bottom lip and made herself breathe. "I can work anywhere."

He took her hand. "Hungry?"

"A little."

"I'm starved, but I'm not cooking and neither are you. I have a drawer full of menus in the kitchen," he said, leading her back downstairs. "We can order something and have it delivered." He pushed through the swinging door of the kitchen.

Lee Ann hopped up on one of the bar stools at the island counter and hooked her legs around the stems. The dishwasher hummed in the background.

"Trying to clean up for company," she teased, lifting her chin in the direction of the washer.

He cut a quick look at her before pulling open the drawer. "Yeah. My mama raised me right." He shut the drawer and came to her with a handful of choices. "You decide. Whatever you want." He sat down for a minute then got right back up. He went to the fridge. "Thirsty?"

"Some juice or cold water is fine."

He took out a jug of filtered water, got two glasses from the overhead cabinet and poured for each of them.

Lee Ann was going over a Mexican menu. "Ever try them? How's the food?"

"Pretty good." He got back up and put the extra menus away. His eyes darted to the dishwasher as if he expected it to spill its contents and point a finger right at him.

"Let's go up front."

"Are you okay?"

"Yeah. Why?"

"I don't know. You seem jumpy or distracted all of a sudden."

"Naw. I'm good." He walked ahead of her.

Lee Ann frowned for a moment then shook it off. *Look for trouble, and you won't have to look far,* she could hear her mother say.

Preston turned on the stereo, pressed the CD button, and the sexy crooning of Kem moved across the room.

Lee Ann settled down on the couch. "I saw him in concert at the Essence Festival a few years ago. I've been in love with his music ever since."

"The brother is no joke." He sat beside her and draped his arm around her shoulder. "You decide what you want?"

Lee Ann turned into his arm, leaned her head on his chest. "That's what I've been thinking about all day—what I want."

"What did you come up with?" He traced the shell of her ear.

"That I want my own life."

"I don't understand."

She thought about how she could explain, what words to choose so that she didn't sound like an idiot.

"Last night—" her lashes fluttered "—was the first time that I stayed out all night, something that grown women do all the time. I know it sounds crazy, but for me it was an anomaly. My sisters left messages, texts, my father threatened to come back to Baton Rogue if I didn't show up by morning." She shook her head, embarrassed to have to tell him all this, but it needed to be said. He had to understand that, to her, what was happening between them was important enough to disrupt and defy the family that she loved and adored.

"The first time?" He echoed the words, and the implication was not lost on him. He drew her closer.

Lee Ann studied her hands.

Preston lifted her head with the tips of his fingers. "Look at me."

Her eyes met his.

"For you to do what you did," he stopped and started again. "That means something. I never had that. Since I was a kid, I pretty much did what I wanted. My mom was too busy trying to keep a roof over our heads to notice." He rocked his jaw. "Look, there are going to be times when we're going to want to be together. And I'm going to want your full attention and not have you worried about what your family is thinking."

She flinched.

"No, listen." He drew her attention back. "That means that we're in this together. I have to get used to this family thing, and you have to be up-front with them."

Her shoulders relaxed. "I'm already working on that."

He grinned, kissed her softly on the lips. "Then the rest is easy."

Chapter 8

Preston stretched, his long, lean body, defined against the fitted white T-shirt. Lee Ann tried to keep her mind on finishing her tortilla and not thinking about the delights beneath that shirt.

"I'm stuffed."

"Me, too." She took their plates from the table and before Preston had a chance to react, she'd opened the dishwasher.

For an instant, he froze.

"You know you waste a lot of water just washing two glasses." She took them out and put them on the counter. "Makes more sense to get a full load and do it all at once." She lined up the plates on the rack and dropped the forks in the holder and shut the door. She turned to him and couldn't place the strained look on his face. "I'm sorry. I don't need to tell you how to wash dishes." She sputtered a nervous laugh. "Old habits."

"You have a lot of work to do?" he asked, changing the subject.

"It shouldn't take long. I need to go over my notes for tomorrow."

"How long have you been teaching?"

"Off and on for about six years. This year I have a poli-sci class. Freshman."

"One of my majors. Maybe I'll drop in one day and see you do your thing."

"Don't you dare!"

He walked up to her and pulled her close. "And why is that?"

His voice dipped down to her center and made it swirl. "I wouldn't be able to concentrate," she managed to say while his hands moved up and down her spine. Her fingers splayed across his chest.

"So if I sat in the room with you and did this…" He kissed her slow and sweet, flicked his tongue across her lips. "Or this…" the pads of his thumbs grazed her waist and moved up to the underside of her breasts. "You wouldn't be able to concentrate?"

She swallowed. Her breathing escalated. "No…"

"Hmm." He pressed against her, letting her feel what she was doing to him. "Then I guess I should let you get to work…so that you can finish as soon—" he kissed her "—as possible." He took her mouth, savored the taste of her mixed with hot spices, pulling her as close to his body as space would allow. She felt like heaven on earth in his arms, and every fiber of him wanted to hold on to it, take her to bed and love her until she begged him to stop.

He pulled back, his eyes so dark and stormy when he

looked at her that a shiver of fearful expectation rushed through her. He brushed his finger along her cheek. "The office is through there," he managed to say.

Preston got her set up and then stretched out on the small tan lounge chair while she worked. His long legs hung over the edge.

"How many students do you have?"

"Hmm, twenty," she murmured, scanning the document on the screen.

"Big class."

"Yes," she added absently, typing data onto the spreadsheet. She checked her handwritten notes.

"What's the lesson for tomorrow?"

"Ethics."

He shifted his body. His conversation with Charlotte replayed in his head. He sat up then stood, walked to the window then back to the lounge. "Hot topic these days."

"Hmm." She glanced over her shoulder. "Are you okay?"

He halted his pacing. "Yeah. I'm going to take a shower and let you work. Come on up when you're done." He walked out.

Lee Ann followed him with her eyes, but his broad back revealed nothing.

Preston pulled off his shirt and dug in the pocket of his shorts to empty them. He pulled out Anthony Paulsen's business card. *Ethics.* He shoved the card in the side pocket of his carryall and went into the shower.

He had some decisions to make in the next few days. The hot, sudsy water slid across the sculpted muscles of his chest, sloshing over the ripples of his stomach before bathing his crotch and flowing between rock-hard thighs. He lathered the navy cloth again. He was torn about meeting with Paulsen. He knew all about those backroom meetings behind closed doors. They were the status quo in politics. As much as the public was led to believe that votes were cast and decisions were made on the floor of the House and the Senate, the real decisions were made over lunch, on golf courses and thousand-dollar-per-plate dinners.

When he entered politics, walking the picket lines and leading community forums, he was an idealist, taught at the feet of the current president when he'd interned for him in Chicago. He believed that if you were honest and passionate and kept the interests of the people at the forefront, you could move mountains. When he was elected senator, he maintained that ideal—that he had the power to change things. It didn't take long for those ideals to be crushed.

The machine of Washington was a behemoth steeped in tradition, old boy networks and under-the-table dealings. The real power in Washington professed change and progress, but it's not what they really wanted. That would mean giving up the power that they believed was rightfully theirs.

So those like him who still had a little milk on their breath tried for as long as they could until opportunities like Paulsen came along and you found yourself tempted by the devil.

"How 'bout some company?"

The soap slipped from his hands.

Lee Ann giggled and stepped in. "Sorry, I didn't mean to scare you."

Preston turned away from the water. His heart raced as much from Lee Ann's surprise appearance as from the irrational idea that she had read his thoughts.

He wiped water from his face and laughed. "Dangerous sneaking up on a naked man." He reached out and ran a single finger down the center of her breasts to her navel. Her stomach quivered beneath his finger.

She bent down and retrieved the fallen soap, and it was the craziest, sexiest move he'd ever seen. Arousal pumped, stiffening him.

Lee Ann held the soap in her palm. The pulsing water made her curves glisten.

"I think you dropped this." Her hazel eyes had turned a warm brown. She began rubbing the soap in slow circles on his chest, his stomach. She bent and rubbed the soap along his inner thighs and was rewarded with a salute. She moved the soap up and down his extended shaft in maddening slow motion.

Preston gritted his teeth and pressed his palm against the cool tile wall to keep himself steady. His thighs trembled. She increased the speed, alternating between her hands and the soap until Preston was sure he would explode.

He captured her wrist. Her gaze flew up to his, and she shuddered. He pulled her to her feet. "Your turn." He took the soap from her that had become an aphrodisiac and began massaging every inch of her body until she whimpered in submission.

Preston dropped what had become a lethal weapon on the floor and pulled Lee Ann to him, letting the water cascade over their bodies. He lowered his head and took a sweet nipple into his mouth. Lee Ann's knees wobbled, and she clung to him, offering up what he sought.

His right hand slid down between her wet, slippery thighs and caressed her until her clit was hard and swollen. Reaching behind him, he turned off the water, pushed the curtain aside, pulled the towel down from the hook and wrapped her in it. Then he picked her up and carried her to his bedroom.

He placed her on the center of the bed and loosened the towel. For several moments, he stood above her and drank her in. She was so perfect. So beautiful. He wanted to take forever with her, but just standing there looking at her had him on the brink of climax.

Lee Ann parted her thighs, and Preston nearly lost his mind. He lowered himself onto the bed and stretched out beside her and began to place tiny kisses on her cheek, the hollow of her neck, the rise of her breasts, down the valley of her stomach.

She writhed and sighed softly as the pleasure intensified. Her head spun. Even her fingertips tingled. Her eyes flew open. She grabbed his shoulder. "Wait."

He lifted his head. "What's wrong?"

She scrambled off the bed and went to her bag. With shaky fingers, she found her makeup pouch and took out a condom and came back to bed. She sat in the middle and handed it to him.

The corner of his mouth curved. "Will you do the honors?"

"I…" She swallowed.

He tore the pack open with his teeth and pulled out the thin sheath. He covered her hand with his and guided her as the covering unrolled along his length. Preston groaned from the bottom of his soul and had to think about monster trucks to keep from losing it.

Lee Ann smiled demurely at her handiwork and scooted back on the bed. "No more waiting," she whispered.

Preston crawled up the bed, and in a long single thrust, he buried himself inside her, shoving all the air out of her lungs and into the room in a shuddering gasp.

He slipped his arms beneath her, wanting every inch of her to be a part of him.

Tonight she wasn't a caretaker, she thought as she raised her hips to meet his every need. Not an event coordinator, hostess or someone else's assistant. He went deeper. Tonight she was a desirable woman with wants and needs and a man willing to fulfill them. "Ohhhh." Tonight nothing else mattered but Lee Ann and Preston. She gripped his shoulders as ecstasy swept through her. Her body arched. The woman behind the layers of responsibility was being stripped bare with every kiss, every caress, every whisper of her name, every groan from his lips. Tonight she was free.

They'd used up half of the supply that she'd brought with her and would have gone further if they hadn't knocked over the clock and realized that it was nearly two in the morning.

Laughing and weak, they curled up together beneath the sheet. Lee Ann rested her head on Preston's chest.

"You are totally out of control, miss," he teased, kissing the top of her head.

"Me! Who was the one who said let's try it standing up?"

"It was fun though, wasn't it?" He lightly pinched her bottom.

She swatted at his hand. "Yeah, it was," she admitted, a shiver running through her, remembering how he'd lifted her in his arms and loved her until they both tumbled onto the bed, spent and happy. Her eyes fluttered closed.

"Get some rest, Lee," he whispered to her.

She nodded, already dozing, and the last thought she had before she slipped into sleep was that she hoped Preston was everything she believed that he was.

They both overslept, and it was Lee Ann who jumped up and shook Preston awake.

He mumbled and pulled the sheet over his head.

She shook him harder. "It's six-thirty."

"Huh," he grumbled and reached for her.

"Wake up, Press. You're going to miss your flight."

He squinted at the clock then at Lee Ann, whose short, spiky hair was a mess all over her head. Her bare breasts were still swollen, and her nipples were standing at attention. He snatched her around the waist and pulled her down. "We have plenty of time," he said and nibbled her neck.

A wave of heat shot through her. "No, we don't," she said unconvincingly as he suckled a nipple. "Pres... aggg...you're going to miss your flight."

He moved above her and pushed her thighs apart with

a swipe of his knee. He leaned across her and took the last condom from the nightstand. "And I won't see you for three weeks," he said, rolling the covering down as far as it would go. He looked into her eyes before draping her legs over his arms. "So what do you say?" He pressed against her opening. "Yes." He teased across the threshold. Her hips instinctively rose. "Or no." He moved in just enough to let her feel him.

She wrapped her arms around his neck. "Yes."

"Woman, you can drive me to the airport any day," he said as Lee Ann swerved into an available space, having turned a forty-five-minute drive into a half hour.

"I'd rather not have to leap over tall buildings in the process," she joked. "Now go on. You really will miss your flight and I have a class."

He leaned across the gears, slipped his hand behind her head and kissed her from the bottom of his soul, leaving them both breathless.

"I'll call you tonight."

Lee Ann nodded. The words stuck in her throat.

He pecked her lips again, opened the door and grabbed his bag from the backseat. He poked his head in the window. "Drive safe."

"I will."

He strode off, swinging his bag by his side. He got to the revolving doors and stopped, turned around and jogged back to the car.

"What's wrong? Did you forget something?"

"Yeah. I forgot to tell you that…I'm crazy about

you." Before she could react, he turned away and was swallowed up with travelers.

Lee Ann sat in the spot so long that security had to inform her that she had to leave.

Chapter 9

"Ethics is our topic for today." Lee Ann began walking across the front of the classroom. "Society assumes when we elect our officials into office that they will follow the law and a moral code and will not allow outside forces to influence their decisions, which should be based on the will of the people. Please open your texts to page 156."

Lee Ann turned the discussion over to the class as they debated points, and her thoughts drifted back to Preston and his parting words. Her pulse quickened. *Crazy about her.* Was he saying that and meaning it or saying it only because he thought he should? Everything was happening so fast. Everything that she'd done since she met Preston had been so out of character for her. Until recently, she never thought she had a spontaneous bone in her body.

"Professor... Professor Lawson..."

Lee Ann blinked. "Yes?"

"Our next class…"

"Oh, I'm sorry. Yes. See you all on Wednesday."

The class started filing out, some giving surreptitious looks over their shoulder.

Lee Ann was off balance. She'd never lost focus in class. How long had she been daydreaming? she worried as she packed up her briefcase. She waited until her students were gone before she walked out.

"Hey, Lee Ann."

Lee Ann turned. Her eyes widened, and a smile moved across her mouth. "Teresa! When did you get back?"

They hugged.

"Today is my first day."

"You look fabulous. How is the new baby?"

"Oh, she's wonderful. I hated to leave her but…" She shrugged. "Have to pay the bills and with John being out of work…"

Lee Ann put her hand on Teresa's shoulder. "I know. It's hard all over. He'll find something."

"That's what I keep telling him. The only good thing about coming off maternity leave is that I can leave Zoie with her dad. Are you finished for the day?"

"Yeah, just my one class."

"There's something different about you." She angled her head and looked Lee Ann over.

Lee Ann frowned. "Different?"

"I don't know—brighter, happier."

Lee Ann laughed. "Okay, I guess that's a good thing."

"So who is he?" she asked in a pseudo whisper.

Lee Ann's face heated. "He?"

"Yes, *he*. Having a new man in a woman's life always makes her glow."

She did feel as if she was beaming inside. She felt new and vibrant. "I have been seeing someone," she confessed. "It's still new, and I don't know where it's going. I just hope that it does," she said breathlessly.

"That is so wonderful for you, Lee." She squeezed her hand.

Teresa had been around during Maxwell and that whole fiasco. She'd encouraged Lee Ann to get back out in the world, but Lee Ann didn't heed her advice. Instead, she became consumed by family and work and duty.

"Is he cute?" she hedged, nudging Lee Ann in the side as they walked toward the exit.

Lee Ann sighed. "Gorgeous."

Teresa giggled and hooked her arm through Lee Ann's. "Now that's what I'm talking about."

They crossed to the parking lot, chatting about new mommyhood and the spring semester.

"Good to have you back," Lee Ann said when they came to a stop in front of her car.

"No, it's good to have you back." She kissed her cheek and walked off to her car.

Lee Ann opened her car door and scooted behind the wheel. She watched Teresa pull out and waved goodbye; a pang of sadness settled in her center. She'd never had to worry about money for bills or having to do without. She believed in what her father and Preston were working toward. It was crucial that they were successful in turning things around for all the people like Teresa. And she, as a teacher, could instill in her students, the future leaders, the importance of working for the people and the good of all. She put the car in Reverse and backed out of her space.

Moving along with the early afternoon traffic, she thought about Teresa's comment. Was it really that obvious that she'd checked out of the excitement of everyday life? She crossed the intersection. Then she was long overdue.

Preston opened the door to his one-bedroom apartment in Dupont Circle. He loved the neighborhood, the shops and the close proximity to the Capitol without being too close. Here he could at least have the illusion of getting away while he was in town.

The setup was simple. There was no pool or backyard grill, but it was comfortable. The eat-in kitchen was small and functional. He had the basics in the sunken living room: couch, loveseat and side chair in a deep hunter-green leather and wood coffee and end tables. Everything was on one floor. That took a bit getting used to. He'd looked for a duplex but hadn't found one in the area that appealed to him.

He strolled through the open space down the short hallway. His bedroom was on the left, and the bath was on the opposite side of the hall. He tossed his mail on the desk by the window and saw the flashing light on his answering machine. He hardly got any calls on the landline unless it was Merna with a problem at the house in Baton Rouge. He pressed the flashing button.

"Preston, Senator Lawson. I assume you must be on your way. I've made reservations for dinner at eight.

There are some issues I want to discuss with you before the session in the morning. I'll see you at Merlot on 16th Street at eight."

Preston blew out a breath. A meeting with the senator certainly wasn't on his agenda for the evening, but he couldn't very well not show up. He stripped out of his clothes. He still had a few hours to get his mind right to meet the senator. But his first order of business was calling Lee Ann.

Her cell phone chirped as she pulled into the driveway of her home. She reached for her phone.

"Hey, Lee."

She filled with warmth. "Hey. You made it." She put the car in Park. "How was the trip?"

"Fortunately uneventful." He chuckled. "What about you? How was your day?"

"Well, for some reason I completely zoned out during class. It seemed I couldn't keep my mind on the topic."

"What was your mind on?"

"Things that had no business being in a class-room."

He heard the joy in her voice. "Well, we'll have to talk about that some more tonight."

"Promise?"

"Promise."

She picked up her briefcase from the passenger seat and got out of the car. "What are your plans for tonight?"

"Actually, I got a message from your father."

Her heart jumped. "About what?"

"He says he wants to discuss some things with me before the session tomorrow."

"Oh." Her thoughts went in a dozen different directions. She knew her father. All of his agendas were laden. And it took work to strip everything away to get to the real issue. "Let me know how it goes."

"I will. I have a few things to take care of, so I'll give you a call tonight."

"Okay. I'll talk to you later."

"Bye."

She disconnected the call and walked up the steps to her front door and went inside. Under other circumstances she wouldn't give a second thought to a meeting between Preston and her father. But the dynamics had changed, and she only hoped that her father would play the senator and not her daddy.

She pressed the phone to her chest as she climbed the steps to her room. Tonight couldn't get there fast enough.

Preston adjusted his tie as he walked into the dimly lit opulence of Merlot. The five-star restaurant was the epicenter of political meetings. At any time one could find any number of congressman and senators, CIA, FBI, corporate heads, economists, lobbyists and of course the Secret Service.

He walked up to the hostess podium. "Preston Graham. I'm meeting Senator Lawson."

The polished young woman checked her register. "Yes, right this way, Senator Graham." She picked up a menu. "Please follow me."

Jacketed waiters moved expertly and unobtrusively

around the linen topped tables. Preston recognized several faces and offered discrete nods. The hostess led him to a private table partitioned with beveled glass. She placed the menu on the table. "Enjoy your evening."

"Senator," Preston greeted as he unbuttoned his jacket and sat down.

Branford barely looked up from the documents in front of him. "Graham." After several moments of tense silence, he closed the folder and slid his half-framed glasses from his nose and set them next to his dinner plate. "How was the flight?"

"Fine, sir."

Branford nodded as if that was the most important bit of information he'd gathered all day. His eyes, identical to Lee Ann's, bored into Preston's. But that was typical of him, his trademark, and what made him so popular among his colleagues and constituents. He had the ability to make one believe that they and their issues were all very personal to him.

The waiter approached. "Can I get you something to drink, sir?" he asked Preston.

"Bourbon, on the rocks."

"Right away."

"Anything else for you, sir?"

"A refill on this scotch."

The waiter nodded his head and moved away as quietly as he'd appeared.

Branford focused on Preston. "Tomorrow's session is crucial," he said without preamble. "As chairman of the subcommittee on the Gulf Restoration, I need to make sure that I have everyone on board."

"Of course, sir."

"I understand you visited the wetlands."

Preston's eyes flashed for a second before he reached for his glass of water. "Yes, I did." He wasn't going to speculate on how he knew.

"I appreciate your proactive approach. It's important that the people know that we are still invested in what's going on down there." He lifted his glass to his lips. "I know that you're working on the education reform bill, as well."

"Yes, sir."

"It's a lot for a junior senator, especially during a first term."

Preston leaned forward. "What are you getting at, sir?"

The waiter returned with their drinks. "Can I take your dinner orders now?"

"I'll have my usual," Branford said.

"And for you, sir?"

"Make that two," Preston said, handing back the menu.

"Two?" Branford raised a bushy brow as the waiter moved away.

"I figure if it's good enough to be your usual, it's good enough for me." He sipped from his drink.

Branford tossed his head back and laughed a rumbling laugh that was infectious. He shook his head as his chuckle diminished. He wagged a thick finger at Preston. "You have balls. That's what I like about you. And your drive. I was just like you when I started out more than three decades ago." He clasped his hands in front of him, twisted his lips for a moment before he continued. "I think you have what it takes, Preston."

"What it takes, sir?"

"Yes. Do you understand what I'm saying?"

Preston leaned back and took Branford in. "I'm not going to guess."

The corner of Branford's mouth flickered. "That's exactly what you should have said. This business we're in," he said, leaning forward, "is full of innuendos and people not saying what they mean. The key to staying ahead of the play is to get people on the record." He jabbed his finger on the table to punctuate his point. "Make them commit." He rolled his wide shoulders. "In eight years, if you play your cards right, stay on the right side of the issues, keep your face in the public light, you will be our Democratic candidate for president of the United States."

Preston blinked back his surprise. Just hearing the words coming from the mouth of Senator Lawson was as close to a confirmation as he would ever get. His temples pounded, and he could hear the blood rushing through his veins.

"To do that, you can't owe anyone, be in anyone's pocket. There will be those who are going to do their damnedest to woo you, line your pockets and once you get in bed with them you'll never get out." He shook his head vigorously.

Did he know about Paulsen the same way he knew about his visit to the wetlands?

"You need to start now, defining where you stand on the issues, not just today's issues but into the future and the long-term implications of your decisions."

The waiter appeared with their meal. Seared sea bass, with basil and lemon over saffron rice.

"Hope you like sea bass," Branford said with a wink. He sliced into his fish, took a mouthful and hummed with pleasure.

Preston tried to concentrate on his meal, but he barely tasted it.

"What are your thoughts about what I've said?"

Preston looked at Branford. "I'm honored, and I know that your belief in me is not misplaced."

"I've watched you for years. From your days in Chicago with the president, coming back to Louisiana, running for office and beating a long-term incumbent." He chewed thoughtfully. "And I know that my daughter chose wisely."

Preston's stomach tightened.

"I wanted to see what you did when I tossed you that ultimatum. You followed your own mind. You didn't get intimidated by the old man." He smiled. "That's the kind of man the country needs and what Lee Ann deserves."

"Thank you, sir."

"But trust me on this," he said, pointing his knife at Preston, "you mess up on the floor or in my daughter's life and I guarantee I will ruin you."

Preston watched Branford work through his dinner with the same precision in which he ran the Senate, his life and his family and didn't doubt his statement.

Chapter 10

Preston returned to his apartment near ten o'clock, still shaken by his conversation with Branford. In the deep recesses of his soul, he'd imagined the day that he would run for higher office. To have someone as powerful as Branford Lawson endorse, even encourage, that idea left him awed. But it didn't come without strings. Nothing did. Every move he made in the coming weeks, months and years would be scrutinized. Beginning with his position on the direction the education reform bill would take—a position that was in opposition to Branford's.

He pulled his tie from his neck and tugged off his jacket. Not to mention his growing relationship with Lee Ann. What if it didn't work out? Would his career be destroyed as a result? If he went against Branford and the party on issues that he disagreed with, would that be held against him, as well? Branford implied as much even as he lauded him for being his own man.

He dropped down on the side of his bed. *President of the United States*. Perhaps only the second recognized African American to hold that office. Eight years was a lot of time for things to change.

Preston picked up the remote from the side of the bed and pointed it at the television, tuning to *Anderson Cooper 360*, who was interviewing those in attendance at a community meeting in a Baton Rouge parish hit hard by the economy and hurricanes. More than half of the schools in the parish were still operating out of makeshift trailers, and the health department had closed two more school buildings as health hazards, putting teachers out of work and hundreds more students with no place to go.

As he watched the angry and mentally beaten parents and disillusioned children, all the victims of a government that had totally failed them, he knew that he had the opportunity to bring major relief and change and hope, with one meeting with Paulsen. But at what cost? The future of a generation now or a possible presidency later? That was the question he wrestled with.

He turned off the television, picked up the phone and called Lee Ann.

"Hey," she whispered in the phone, the edges of sleep making her voice throaty and enticing.

Just hearing her on the other end loosened the knots that had formed in his gut during the past few hours.

"Did I wake you?"

"I was waiting for your call." She turned on her side. "How was dinner?"

"Interesting to say the least."

"Is that good or bad?"

He exhaled a long breath. "I, uh, need to talk to you about some things, but I'd rather do it face-to-face."

Lee Ann pushed herself into a sitting position. "Is something wrong?"

"No, nothing's wrong." He blew out a breath. "Everything is fine. Just some things have come up, and I have some decisions to make. I'll say this. Your father, in his own unique way, approves of our relationship."

"He does?"

"He told me as much. Along with his belief that in eight years I'll be in a position to run for office."

Her pulse picked up. "Office?" she asked, not daring to say what she thought.

"Yes, presidential office."

"Preston…he said that?"

"He did."

"I mean just out of the blue?"

"Not exactly. It was all part of a larger conversation that had to do with making the right choices and allies."

She was quiet for a moment. "My father never says anything lightly or without careful thought," she said slowly. "He has a lot of confidence in you, and his support will go a very long way."

"I know."

"You should be ecstatic. Do you know how many young senators would kill to be in your position right now?"

How could he tell her that as much as he was stunned by her father's declarations he was also stymied by it? For as much as her father professed that he admired him being his own man, at the same time, couched in his praise, was the underlying idea that he could never be his own man as long as he went along with Branford Lawson. Not to mention the fate that would befall him if things didn't work out with him and Lee Ann.

"I guess I'm still in shock," he finally said.

"It is a lot to digest. But Preston, your future has taken on a new direction. The possibilities..." She halted. "Is it even what you want?"

"I've thought about it. I suppose a lot of people in politics have thought about it. But I never said it out loud or admitted that it was a viable long-term goal."

"Now it is, and I think you are going to have to get used to it."

"I guess I will." He paused. "So enough about me. Let's talk about us."

"Yes. Let's..."

"I was thinking that with our schedules being what they are we won't have a great deal of time to spend together."

"I know. I was thinking the same thing. With you being in Washington half the year..."

"But we're both off for the spring recess, me here at the Senate and you with your classes."

"Yes..."

"I know this may seem kind of soon, but what do you think about getting away together, taking a trip?"

"A trip?"

"Yes, a mini vacation. Go someplace where no one knows us. We can relax, get waited on, enjoy each other." He paused, waited for her response that didn't come. "How does that sound?"

"Preston...I..."

"You think it's too soon. I understand." He was unexpectedly disappointed.

"No…yes…I've never been away with a man before. I mean not like that," she blurted out. "I know it sounds sophomoric but…I've never wanted to."

An inkling of hope stirred. "Do you want to now?"

"Well…" She drew in a breath, remembering what Teresa said earlier about her deserving more than the life she was living. Everything about her was rational and organized and responsible. But since Preston had come into her life, she'd begun to shed all of the restraints, and it was scary and thrilling at the same time. And she liked it.

"Yes, I do! Did you have some place in mind?"

Preston's insides felt as if they were smiling as much as he was. "I was thinking something tropical…"

The morning session began at ten. There were hundreds of pages of documents to read through and make adjustments and additions to. And it seemed to Preston that everyone on the education committee had a different opinion, each wedded to their own districts and self-interests. By the time they broke for lunch, everyone walking out of the room knew that the new legislation would never pass before the spring recess. They'd been at it for weeks and were no further along than when they started. To Preston it felt as if they'd gone backward instead of forward. His head was pounding. Well, if the wheels of justice grinded slowly, Preston mused, irritated and annoyed, then the wheels of government were at a standstill. It was no wonder that the people were fed up with business as usual.

He turned down the corridor, intent on going out for some air and to clear his head.

"Senator Graham."

He turned to the sound of his name. Anthony Paulsen began walking toward him.

This he didn't need.

Anthony stuck out his hand when he came to a stop in front of Preston. "Anthony Paulsen."

With great reluctance he shook his hand. "Yes, I know who you are."

He didn't flinch from the cold shoulder. "We have an acquaintance in common. I was hoping that her conversation with you would have sparked a conversation between us."

The corridors were beginning to fill as the meeting and conference rooms began to empty their occupants.

"I'm heading out for lunch. Can we walk and talk?"

He fell in step next to Preston. "Certainly."

They walked out into the early afternoon. The White House stood in the distance.

"Charlotte speaks very highly of you."

"Does she." It was more of a statement than a question.

"She feels that you would be amenable to support from many of my connections. The kind of support we are willing to offer will turn things around in your district. I know how invested you are in education reform and the platform that you stood on during election." He hooked a finger over his shoulder indicating the building they'd left. "They won't let that happen—not even members of your own party. But if you have the money, and the corporate muscle behind you, you can get it done."

Preston stopped walking. He turned and looked into the cunning eyes. He knew that Paulsen was as good as his word. If he said he could get things done, he would.

"It was good talking to you," Preston said. "I've really got to go."

"Think about what I'm saying. Think about the good you could do. Think about what your success would mean for your career." He stepped back. "You have my number. Think about it and give me a call." He turned and walked away in the opposite direction.

For several moments, Preston stood at the bottom of the steps of the Capitol. *The choices you make. Be your own man. The choices you make. Your future. Eight years.* The words ran circles in his head.

"It's great to see you looking really happy, sis," Dominique said, as she sat with Lee Ann going over the details for a grant that Dominique was working on for the foundation several weeks later.

Lee Ann glanced up from the notes. "Really?" She grinned. "Did I look unhappy before?"

"No, not unhappy…" She searched for the word. "Resigned, I guess. Yeah, resigned. As if some part of you had simply accepted life and wasn't looking for anything else."

Lee Ann's brows rose and fell. "Wow. I never thought of it that way."

Dominique put down her pen and pushed the notebook aside. "After Maxwell, you changed."

Her body momentarily stiffened. "I had reason to change."

"Of course you did. You were hurt. But...it was almost like you never got over it. And then Mom got sick, and you took on the world to get away from the hurt."

She'd never said the words out loud, but she knew that's how she felt and what she had done. The past few years had turned her into a different person, someone who lived her life through others because she was still afraid of her own life. She was slowly beginning to trust her feelings again. She was entrusting her heart bit by bit to Preston. And although they were miles away it made them work even harder at their relationship. Preston had made several weekend visits since he'd had to return to Washington and even surprised her one afternoon showing up on her doorstep because he had the following day off. Those brief times that they were able to spend with each other were intense and maddeningly thrilling and only increased their desire to be together. She was looking forward to their trip to Cancun. Recess couldn't come fast enough.

She thought about him all the time, and from the middle-of-the-day text messages that he sent and the late night phone calls that they shared, Lee Ann was confident that Preston felt the same way.

Dominique reached out and touched Lee Ann's hand. "I'm glad you have Preston. He brought you back." She twirled the pen in her hand. "What did Daddy have to say about your trip to Cancun?"

Lee Ann chuckled. "Oddly enough, he seemed not to mind. Only thing he said was be discrete. There was no reason for me and Preston to become someone's headlines.

"I can only imagine what they would turn that into. But I don't even think the press would want to get on Daddy's bad side."

"That's true. But we're still trying to keep things low-key. Besides, Preston doesn't need the distraction with all that he has going on. He says the bill won't pass before the recess even with all the work they've done."

"I know, and from all reports, the president isn't happy."

"That's an understatement." She glanced at the figures on the pages in front of her. "I really appreciate you helping me with this grant, Lee."

"Sure." She checked some information on her computer screen.

"I would have never gotten First Impressions off the ground without your help." She folded her slender hands on top of each other. "I know that Daddy thinks that what I do is nice but that's it. He would have given me the money to build buildings and fill them if that's what it took. But I wanted him to see that I could do something on my own. So that he would take me seriously."

"Dom…"

She shook her head. "No, it's true. He only sees Rafe, the heir apparent, and you. Even Desiree and Justin get his attention." She uttered a sad laugh. "You don't know how hard it is sometimes being the carbon copy of someone else and never having your own identity. Desi was always quiet, smarter in school, the responsible one.

Me, just the opposite. I wanted to be noticed for me, not because I look just like someone else."

"Dom, no one thinks of you that way."

"Of course they do. And I did it to myself for years. Part of me likes it, but at the root of it all, I just want him to love me for me." A tear slid down her cheek. "After Mama, Rafe and you, it seems like he didn't have any more love left."

Lee Ann's heart seemed to twist in her chest. She got up from her chair and came around to Dominique. She knelt down in front of her. "Dom, listen to me."

Dominique looked up through tear-filled eyes.

"Daddy can be a hard man. We all know that. But don't ever doubt for a minute his love for you." She squeezed her hands. "Do you think he would fuss you out as much if he didn't care? He thinks you're wild and frivolous because that's the way you act, sweetie. You have no idea how proud he is of what you've accomplished."

"Proud? He never tells me."

"I know. But he tells me."

Dominique blinked in amazement. "What does he say?"

"That the work you are doing is important. He knew you had it in you if you put your mind to it. He wanted to finance the whole thing, but he knew that you needed to do it yourself."

"He said that?"

Lee Ann nodded.

Dominique wiped her eyes. "I never knew."

"Now you do. And if you ever say that I told you, I will deny it on a stack of Bibles." She grinned.

Dominique sputtered a laugh. "Okay." She sniffed.

Lee Ann slowly stood. "How about if you use some of your skills and help me shop for some outfits for my trip?"

Dominique brightened. "Now you're talking."

For the past few weeks, Preston had done everything within his power to avoid Charlotte. She'd left numerous messages—none of which he'd returned. Anthony had called, as well. The pressure was beginning to get to him, and there had been moments when he was a phone call away from agreeing to deal with Paulsen. The only thing that kept his head straight was Lee Ann, talking with her, looking forward to the next time they would be together. She'd unwittingly become his conscience. He didn't want to do anything that would tarnish her view of him, even if it meant him forgoing what could easily make him the hero of the Gulf.

He wanted to tell her about Charlotte and Anthony and the opportunity that was being placed at his feet. But he couldn't, so he talked to the one other person in the world that he trusted, Paul.

"If you do this, agree to letting them support you, you'll be indebted to them for the long haul," Paul had said over drinks the prior night.

"I know. But if I do, thousands of children will have a future. Schools will get rebuilt, community schools, my dream. Teachers will be employed and there will be the promise of a better life for everyone."

Paul exhaled. "There has to be another way."

"Yeah, there should be. But if this bill ever gets passed it will never happen. As much as they claim it will revolutionize education, it's nothing more than government takeover. And we know the government has a lousy track record when they take over anything."

"Understatement."

"The president is pushing the reform. But no one can agree on the how."

Paul leaned forward. "Look, you know him. You worked with him. Why don't you arrange for a meeting and talk to him, lay out your plan? That way you don't bump heads on the floor and the decision will come from the man, and you won't be looked at as the holdout, the new upstart."

Preston swirled his drink around. "I'll think about it."

He held his glass toward Preston. "Do."

And he had been all day. He'd been going over the details of his idea. If he could get the funds to begin setting up model schools, it was something that could be replicated across the country. He'd work on setting up a meeting with the president when he got back from Cancun.

Chapter 11

"Excited?" Preston asked as he and Lee Ann took their seats on the plane.

"Very."

"I've been dreaming about this trip for weeks. I want to make it a time you'll never, ever forget." He kissed her lightly on the lips.

"We have a private bungalow on the beach," he whispered in her ear, "a housekeeper who will prepare all our meals, access to all the amenities of the resort, a car at our disposal and all the time we want to spend with each other."

She sighed in delight. "How did you have time to arrange for all of this?"

"I have a great assistant. I told her what I wanted, and she took care of all of the arrangements."

"Well, aren't you a lucky man having women willing to do your bidding," she teased.

He leaned closer and whispered in her ear. "The only woman I'm interested in doing my bidding is you."

A shiver ran through her. "And you know as the daughter of a politician…"

"I know, quid pro quo."

They laughed and held hands as the plane taxied down the runway.

From the moment they stepped off the plane in Mexico, they could feel the energy. Everywhere they looked, bodies glistened and laughter and excitement filled the air.

After clearing customs, they collected their luggage, and Preston had a car waiting that took them directly to their bungalow.

Their house on the beach was everything that Preston said it would be and more. The front was glass from end to end and looked out onto endless beauty. The sandy beaches were blindingly white, and the water was certainly the bluest water in all of the Caribbean.

The layout was open air with one room leading into the other. The master bedroom came complete with a Jacuzzi and a skylight for watching the heavens right over the king-size bed. The furnishings were a cool off-white in a heavy linen fabric and offset by standing plants and splashes of color in turquoise, sunset orange and lemon yellows. It was like walking through paradise.

"It's gorgeous," she said, moving from room to room.

Preston slid up behind her and put his arms around her waist. He turned her to face him. "Nothing compares to you, Lee." He put a finger to her lips when she started to protest. "I know it sounds like a line. But I think you know me well enough by now to know that I say what I believe and what I feel."

She swallowed.

"To me you are the most beautiful, most extraordinary woman I've ever known. And I'm going to spend all week long proving it to you."

Looking at the sincerity in his eyes and hearing it in his voice she realized once again how much Preston had impacted her life and her vision of herself. Lee Ann sunk into the cocoon of his embrace, and for the first time, she said out loud the self-doubts that she'd always lived with.

"My sisters were always considered the beauties of the family—a striking, showstopping duet." She rested her head against his chest and was soothed by the steady beat of his heart. "And my brothers are what women call drop-dead gorgeous. Me, I was always considered the *cute* one."

He tenderly stroked her back, wanting to stop her but knowing that she needed to say what was on her heart.

"Maybe that's why it was so easy for me to fall into the role of caregiver, nurturer, the responsible one. It's what I had to offer."

"Lee Ann, look at me."

She lifted her gaze to meet his. He held her chin in his palm.

"From the moment I saw you that night across the room, something opened up inside of me. There have been women in my life, but I was always too driven by my career and wouldn't invest in anyone long term. Except once."

Her eyes registered surprise.

"Her name is Charlotte Dupree." He released a long sigh. "I guess it's time I told you about that part of my life." He took her hand and led her over to the couch.

Lee Ann's heart was pounding so loud and so fast that she could hardly breathe. Of course he had a life before her. That wasn't it. It was the way he said her name.

Slowly she sat down, not knowing what to expect.

Preston had been contemplating telling her about Charlotte ever since that night in the park and then again when she turned up at his house. But there was a part of him that didn't want to muddy their relationship by even evoking Charlotte's name. It was stupid. And he felt guilty for hiding something that shouldn't be hidden. Now, with Paulsen breathing down his neck, Charlotte wasn't far behind.

"I met Charlotte when I worked in Chicago doing community activist work with the president—well, before he was president. She was at a rally that I'd helped to organize. We started talking, dating… We got engaged."

Lee Ann stiffened.

Preston looked off into the distance. "On the day of our wedding, I got a note from her cousin saying she couldn't marry someone without a future. She was sorry."

"Oh, Preston…" She took his hand.

He shook his head. "It shook me up in ways that I can't even explain. But what it did for me was give me a purpose. Maybe I wanted to prove her wrong. Maybe I wanted to prove something to myself. But I poured myself into my career to the exclusion of everything and everyone else. Getting ahead and winning were the only things that mattered to me—until I met you and I realized how much of life I'd been missing, I was only existing."

She stroked his face. "I know about that kind of hurt, of turning inside yourself and turning the world out." She told him about Maxwell and how devastated she was by what he'd done, how she blamed herself for not being pretty enough, sexy enough, free-spirited enough because in her mind it had to be her shortcomings and not his. "So if at times it seems that it's hard for me to accept the things you say it's because I'm just learning all about a new me, the one that I buried under duty and work and responsibility. The new Lee Ann that you introduced me to."

"And I want to teach you, show you, tell you in every way that I can just how pretty and smart and funny and keep-me-up-all-night sexy you are." He brushed his lips against hers. "And how being with you, having you in my life, has made me want to be better—a better leader, friend, lover, a better man."

He kissed her long and slow and deep to confirm and reaffirm his declaration. Her body yielded to his touch, coming alive beneath his tender exploration.

"How about if we christen our new abode?" he whispered in her ear before dropping hot kisses along her neck.

"I've never made love under a skylight," she said, her breath escaping in short hot bursts.

"Say no more." He scooped her up and carried her off.

* * *

During the day, they did all the touristy things from visiting the Mayan ruins of Tulum, to deep-sea fishing. After much cajoling, kisses and promises of a ravishing night, Lee Ann convinced Preston to rent them both jet skis, which he enjoyed so much he went back the following day. The early evenings were spent nightclub hopping, an entertainment factor that Cancun was known for. Their favorite was Coco Bongo, which offered a mix of music, live shows and could hold up to 3,000 people. And in between it all they talked and learned new things about each other like how Lee Ann was a closet artist and loved to paint in her spare time. Or that Preston wanted to be a tennis player but settled for racquetball. Sometimes she wished she was an only child, and he wished he wasn't. They both missed their mothers but for different reasons, hers through death and his through a lack of a relationship.

"When did you talk to her last?" Lee Ann asked as they snuggled amongst the thick pillows and scented sheets.

"A few weeks ago. I try to stay in touch. Send her money and check to see that she's all right."

She stroked his chest while he talked.

"It's not a typical mother-son relationship. I was pretty much on my own since I was a kid. I mean not so much because my mother wanted it that way but because she had no other choice. She was always working—slaving was more like it. And even though I knew she was doing it so we could eat, a part of me still resented her. Resented her for choosing someone who would leave us."

She kissed his neck. "We can't help who we fall in love with," she said softly. "And we never know how it's all going to turn out."

Preston looked down into her upturned face. "No, we can't help who we fall in love with." His eyes moved slowly over her face. He watched the tiny pulse beat in her throat as he brushed her hair off her forehead. "I'm in love with you, Lee Ann." His own words stunned him in their spontaneity and moved through him like a warm wave that he couldn't explain. "I love you."

Lee Ann's breath caught in her chest. She reached for him and pulled him to her, covering his lips, tasting him, assuring herself that he was real, that his words were real and echoed the same sentiments in her soul.

She found herself beneath him, surrounded by him, ignited from the inside out by his touch. The skimpy teddy that Dominique had convinced her to buy found its way to the floor. To Lee Ann, Preston touched her, whispered to her in ways that he had never done before. There seemed to be a new reference, a newness, as if he was finding her for the very first time and the discovery for the both of them took them to a place they had never been.

They loved slow and gentle, deep and long. Lee Ann clung to him, opening her body to him in ways she'd never done before. He'd always satisfied her, rocked her to her soul. But this time he touched her soul, and the sensation was sublime, lifting her from this earthly place. So sweet, so potent that she wept from a joy so deep it shook her, controlled her, stole her breath and brought her to a climax that was frightening in its magnificence.

He held her with a tenderness that one does with a precious treasure as he moved within her, and her orgasm continued to build and wrap around him, sucking him into her vortex until he shuddered and shared with her every drop of his essence.

They lay together in awed silence of what had transpired between them, both realizing that for all the times that they'd been together they'd had wonderful, incredible, mind-blowing sex that bound them and set a foundation for them to build on. But this was different. This time they truly made love. They discovered in each other what making love really was. It was opening yourself up and letting the other person in. It was giving yourself to another totally without holding back and knowing that you were going to be safe with them.

"Press…"

"Hmm…"

"That's never happened to me before," she said, her voice still dreamy. "I felt as if I left my body."

"I know. So did I." He stroked the curve of her back, still shaken by the experience.

Lee Ann moved closer. "Did you really mean what you said?"

He angled his body so that he could look at her. "Of course I meant it. I never meant anything more. I love you, Lee Ann. And that's a hard thing for me to admit. I didn't think I'd feel love again. But this is different. It's nothing I can compare it with, and I don't want to. This is me and you. Ours."

She needed to hear him say it—have the words stand alone and not be a prelude to what happened between them. Yet even without his admonition she knew it was true. She felt it in the center of her being. And that's why she knew that she could turn her heart over to him and he wouldn't break it.

She cupped his face and stared deep into his eyes. "I love you," she whispered as her heart thundered and her body tingled.

"I know," he said against her mouth, before covering her body with his.

They spent the next few days of their two-week-long getaway combing the shops for souvenirs to bring back home, lounging on the beach, sampling the restaurants, dancing the night away and falling deeper in love.

Long into the night they talked, often sitting out on the beach until the sun rose in brilliant hues of red and gold above the horizon.

But as it grew closer for them to return to the real world, Preston knew that he didn't want to go back and have anything stand between them.

Over dinner he told her everything about Charlotte and the real reason why she'd "looked him up."

"She was at your house while I was talking to you on the phone?"

"Yes."

She thought back to that night months earlier. She looked at him from across the table. "That's why there were only two glasses in the dishwasher." She snorted her disbelief. "Why didn't you just tell me then?"

"I don't know—worried about what you would think, not having things clear in my head."

"Clear in your head? Like what?"

"Like whether or not I was going to take her up on her offer to meet with Paulsen."

Her head jerked back. "You didn't actually consider it, did you?"

His jaw clenched. "The truth?"

"Yes, Preston. The truth."

"Yeah, I did think about it. I thought about it a lot. I know that with the kind of support that Paulsen can provide I can get real change in my district." He looked away. "But I also knew what it would cost me in the long run."

Lee Ann didn't know what to think, what to believe. If he kept something like that from her, what else would he keep from her? How far was he willing to go to get what he wanted?

"Is there anything else I should know?"

"Only that I'm not going to keep anything else from you. I promise you that."

"If there was one thing that I learned in my relationship with Maxwell it was that if we can't be honest with each other then we're doomed."

"It's been a long time for me too, Lee. I haven't had to consider someone else's feelings about what I did in a very long while. It takes some getting used to."

She studied his face. "Are you over her?"

The question was so out of left field that it caught him off guard, making him hesitate a split second too long.

Lee Ann held up her hand. "Never mind. Don't answer." She pushed her plate aside. "I'm tired. I'm ready to go."

Preston wasn't sure what was happening—only that

in the blink of an eye things had made a wrong turn. And for the first time in all the nights that they'd spent together since they'd met, they didn't make love.

He was sure she wasn't asleep even though she hadn't moved a muscle since she got under the covers and pulled the sheet up to her neck. He stared up at the sky twinkling through the skylight. This was their last night together—a lousy ending to a perfect two weeks. She wanted honesty but wouldn't give him the opportunity to be honest. He thought they'd gotten past the whole Charlotte thing until she sprung that question on him. He couldn't understand why she needed to ask. He was with her, not Charlotte.

The more he thought about it, the more pissed off he became. If that's all it took to shake them up, what chance did they have of surviving the real bumps in the road? If she thought that he still had feelings for Charlotte, after everything that she'd done to him, then she didn't know him at all. He flopped over onto his side, giving Lee Ann his back. Fine, if that's the way she wanted it. Fine.

Lee Ann lay curled up in a ball as if wrapping herself up could provide some kind of barricade. She was miserable. Why couldn't he answer her? What was the hesitation in his eyes? Did he really have to think about it? She knew what it was like to wonder "what if?" She'd played that mind game with herself for months—even years—after she and Maxwell broke up. What if I'd been more understanding, taller, better in bed, prettier, funnier, the daughter of someone else. The questions tumbled around in her head until she thought she'd go out of her mind. Did he ever wonder "what if?" when it came to Charlotte? And that question plagued her throughout the night.

The car was in front of the bungalow at 6:00 a.m. ready to take them to the airport. Preston and Lee Ann moved about the space and each other like strangers, only passing the barest of niceties between them. They sat on opposite sides of the limo, staring out of opposite windows, both wondering why things had gone so wrong.

Chapter 12

They'd already planned for the car to drop off Lee Ann at home and take Preston to his place before bringing him to the airport so that he could head right out to Washington. But with their current stalemate the parting seemed much more profound, much more permanent.

Preston helped her with her bags and brought them up to the front door. They stood awkwardly next to each other, neither knowing what to say to make everything all right again.

"You need me to bring those in for you?"

"No. Thanks," she said, hoping that she didn't sound as sad and frightened as she felt. "I can manage."

Preston shoved his hands in his pockets and nodded. "Well, I've got to get going."

She swallowed over the knot in her throat and lowered her head so that he wouldn't see the tears that were threatening to spill. "Okay. Have a safe flight."

He started to touch her.

She held her breath.

Preston turned and strode toward the waiting limo and didn't look back.

Lee Ann knew that she was going to crumble into a million pieces. She needed to get inside, get to her room before she fell apart all over her front steps.

Fighting back tears, she reached for the doorknob just as it was being turned on the side. The door swung open. And when she saw her brother, Rafe, whatever willpower she had to keep from crumbling was lost. She buried her face in his chest and wept.

Instinctively, he wrapped his arms protectively around her. "It's all right. It's all right, cher." His dark eyes flew to scan the property, and it took him a minute to realize that she wasn't hurt, at least not physically. "Come on, let's get you inside."

"My bags," she muttered, wiping at her eyes.

"Forget the bags. They'll be fine. Come on." He shoved the door closed and ushered her into the study on the ground floor and shut the door behind them. "Come on. Sit down. Take a breath."

She bobbed her head and slumped down on the small sofa. Rafe pulled up the office chair and sat in front of her.

"You want to tell me what's wrong?"

"It's…all so stupid," she managed.

"Okay. What's so stupid?"

"Everything," she sniffed.

Rafe's brows rose and fell. He pursed his lips in thought. "You're probably right, but what in particular about everything is stupid?"

"Preston," she blurted out.

Rafe's chest filled. "Did he hurt you?" He clasped her shoulders, shocking her with the intensity of his grip. "Tell me, Lee Ann." His nostrils flared. "I swear, if he hurt you I'll break him in half, I don't give a damn if…"

"Rafe, please. It's not like that."

"Then tell me what it's like, Lee Ann," he said, trying to get a grip on his boiling temper. "I promised him if he even thought about hurting you I—"

"We…I got upset about another woman."

He shook his head in confusion. "Another woman? In Cancun?"

"No." She shook her head and tried to get her thoughts together. She wiped her eyes and folded her hands in her lap. Slowly she told him about the conversation they'd had from start to finish and how he reacted when she'd asked him about Charlotte.

Rafe sat back in the chair and tried to keep from laughing. This wasn't anywhere near as bad as he'd thought. "Darlin', take it from a man who's found himself in all manners of mess with women. Here is a man who has confessed to being in love with you, opening up to you about a woman from his past, telling you that he promises that the future is going to be open and honest and you turn around and ask him is he over some woman that he clearly doesn't care about."

"Then why didn't he tell me in the first place when she showed up?"

"There's something you need to understand about men. There's three things that we do: protect, profess and provide. His not telling you was not to lie to you or him hiding something from you. It was to protect you from that part of his life that hurt him. Men don't ever really want the woman that they care about to see them weak or humbled. And he professed his love to you."

Lee Ann turned it all over in her head. She knew she had overreacted, and it created a snowball effect. The entire thing had gotten blown up out of proportion, and she had no one to blame but herself.

"I told you it was stupid," she said sheepishly.

Rafe chuckled. "Yeah, you did."

"I should call him."

Rafe nodded. "So he's made up his mind about Paulsen?"

"He says he has."

"Do you believe him?"

"Yeah, I do."

"Good. I'd hate to think that he would take the bait. It's not worth it in the long run. It's one of the main reasons I don't want any part of politics. It's a big payola operation."

"But things do get accomplished."

"Yeah." He chuckled. "They get things accomplished in spite of themselves." He stood. "Call him."

"I will."

"And next time give the man a chance. That's what's wrong with women always ready to jump to conclusions," he muttered as he walked out.

Lee Ann sniffed back the rest of her tears, wiped her eyes and tried to figure out what to say to Preston.

The car was waiting for him outside of his house. He dropped his suitcases in the closet, tossed a few things in his carryall, talked with Merna and roughed up Rocky before he headed back out to the airport.

Sitting in the back of the limo he thought about the weeks ahead, the long days and nights, all of them possibly spent without the hope of having Lee Ann at the end of the rainbow.

He wasn't sure what had stopped him from simply telling her that he didn't have feelings for Charlotte. He just couldn't get his mind wrapped around the idea that she would even ask him that after everything he'd said, everything they'd shared, the new place that they'd arrived at. It knocked him for a loop. And she took that hesitation to mean something that it didn't.

The driver took the turn onto the highway leading to the airport. Preston watched the city disappear behind him.

Lee Ann paced the length of her bedroom listening to Preston's phone ring until it went to voice mail. Each time, she hung up. She should leave a message, she kept telling herself, but she didn't. She'd initially tried him at home, hoping to catch him, but Merna said she'd just missed him. She been calling his cell phone ever since.

Frustrated, she tossed her phone on the bed and decided to wait until later and try again. She decided to go through her suitcase and get out the gifts for her sisters before they came home, when she remembered she'd never brought her bags in from the front steps. Hopefully Rafe at least put them in the house on his way out.

She went back downstairs, expecting to see her luggage by the door. She stopped in her tracks.

"Your brother let me in."

"But I thought…you should be at the airport. You'll miss your flight." Her legs shook as she came down the rest of the stairs.

Preston walked to her, meeting her on the bottom step. "I couldn't get on a plane and leave things the way they were between us."

"I'm sorry. It was silly and insecure…"

He put his finger to her lips. "Let me say this now, once and for all. It's over between me and Charlotte. It has been for a very long time. Whatever feelings I had for her, I left in the church years ago." He stepped closer. "I love you. You. And I need you to know that you can trust me—trust me with your secrets, your dreams, your fears, your heart. And I won't betray that trust."

Tears of joyful relief slid down her cheeks.

"Those are happy tears, I hope."

She nodded and wrapped her arms around his neck, bringing her mouth to his, sinking into the security of his embrace, the sweetness of his kiss. Her heart soared. "I love you," she murmured against his mouth.

"Tell me again."

"I love you," she said, tossing her head back, her voice filled with laughter.

Preston held her tighter, kissed her exposed neck. "Now that we have that straight," he said, his breath hot and intoxicating against the length of her neck.

"How much time do you have?" she asked in a thready whisper.

He looked into her eyes, and a slow grin moved across his mouth. "Why?"

"We're the only ones home." She started backing up the stairs.

"I guess I can catch a later flight."

Chapter 13

Preston returned to Washington renewed and determined to rid himself of the albatross of Paulsen and Charlotte before things got out of hand, and also to gain an audience with the president, neither of which would be easy as the commander in chief was managing two wars—the economic war at home and the war on terrorism abroad—and he was relying on the House and the Senate to do their jobs, the ones the people had elected them to do.

He hadn't been back in Washington for a good week when he got a call from Charlotte wanting to know if they could meet for lunch—just to talk.

Do you still have feelings for her? The question continued to haunt him even though the issue was resolved between him and Lee Ann. But he needed to settle it for himself once and for all. He'd agreed to meet her downtown at two at Buddy's, a place they were both familiar with.

When he looked for a parking space at the restaurant, Preston spotted Charlotte seated at one of the outdoor tables. As usual, she looked like she was ready for a photo shoot. He watched her work her show with the waiter, who nearly tripped over himself to get her the drink she'd ordered. There was no question that she was a gorgeous woman. But she had a heart of stone. No soul. Charlotte Dupree would auction off her own mother if she thought it could get her what she wanted.

What was he doing here? Why even risk being seen with her? To prove to himself that he could withstand her charms? Looking at her through untinted eyes, he finally realized that he was over her and what he'd felt for her all those years ago wasn't love but lust. He knew what love was now, and he had no intention of screwing it up.

He pulled into a parking space across the street from where she was seated and got out of the car. Checking traffic, he walked across the street and came up beside her.

She looked up over her dark shades. "There you are. I was beginning to think I'd been stood up."

"I'm not staying. I'm not even sitting."

She frowned. "What are you talking about? I thought we were having lunch."

"No, Charlotte, we're not having lunch. We're not having anything. I let unfinished business with us pull me back into even having a conversation with you. My mistake. It's over, Charlotte. We're done. I don't want or need your so-called help. I don't want your phone calls.

I wish you all the best. I really do. I hope whatever it is you're looking for you eventually find. I finally did." He looked at her, and for a moment he thought he actually saw real hurt in her eyes. "Take care of yourself." He turned and walked away, secure in the knowledge that chapter of his life was finally closed.

When he returned to his office, he took Anthony Paulsen's card from his wallet. He took his cell phone out of his jacket pocket and dialed his number. He answered on the third ring.

"Senator Graham, great to hear from you. I hope you've come to a decision about having us help support your efforts."

"Yes, I have thought about it. The answer is no. I'd rather do things my way."

"But Senator…"

"The answer is no. But I'm sure you'll find someone who is willing to sell their soul. It just happens not to be me." He disconnected the call and suddenly felt like celebrating.

There was a light knock on his door.

"Yes?"

"Senator, the president's scheduling secretary is on the phone."

"Thanks, Denise."

He drew in a steadying breath and waited for his secretary to close the door behind her before he picked up the phone. He cleared his throat.

"This is Senator Graham."

"Good afternoon. The president wants to know if you are available tomorrow at 3:15 p.m.?"

"I'll make myself available."

"Wonderful. I'll let the president know, and we'll see you tomorrow."

Slowly he hung up the phone. This was it. This was his opportunity. He rubbed his jaw. He wasn't going to blow it. He picked up the phone and dialed Paul's number. They agreed to meet at Preston's apartment when Paul finished overseeing the editing of the evening news segment.

"I told you, man," Paul said as he took a long swallow of his Corona. "He already knows you are a man of action. He's seen you and worked with you on the ground. All you have to do is present your plan. It's a winner. It only needs the right backing to make it fly."

Preston smiled. "I know. If we can just get one model into operation," he said, holding up one finger, "it will be replicated across the country."

"Have you told Lee Ann about it?"

"Not yet. I wanted to tell her when I knew something." He focused on the contents of his glass.

"What aren't you telling me?"

"She doesn't really know anything about it."

Paul leaned forward. "Why?"

"Because her father oversees that committee. He's the one who has been pushing for the votes for the current education reform bill to pass. He's worked on it for the past year. If I come in there wanting to turn things around and go against Senator Lawson in the process…"

Paul held up his hand. "I get it. And you seeing his daughter only compounds your problem."

"Exactly." He finished off his beer.

"Well, buddy, a private meeting with the president of the United States doesn't stay 'secret' very long."

Lee Ann walked across the grounds of the college campus intent on getting home and cooling off. It was only the middle of June, and the temperatures had skyrocketed. Fortunately there was only a week left of classes before the summer break. And summer break for her also meant summer break for Preston. She smiled to herself as she approached the parking lot. With so many measures needing to be dealt with in Washington, her and Preston's time together was becoming more and more limited. More often than not he worked so late on Fridays that he couldn't catch a flight out, and leaving on Saturday morning to arrive late afternoon only to turn right back around was exhausting for him at best. So she'd started coming down on Thursday evenings since her last class was Wednesday. It worked out, and she was slowly shedding her cloak of guilt for leaving her sisters and brothers. As Teresa kept reminding her, they were grown, and if they didn't know how to take care of themselves by now then they had a lot more to worry about than her being gone for a couple of days per month.

She would just be glad when they were both free to see each other. Even though they didn't talk about the strain of commuting, it was beginning to wear on them both. Preston had been unusually edgy over the past few days. Their late-night talks were short and often devoid of their passion and promises. Talking to each other late at night was what helped to bridge the distance between them. When she mentioned it to him last night, he told her to hang on. He would tell her everything tonight when they talked.

She couldn't imagine what it was. She deactivated the alarm on her car and was just opening the door when she was stopped by a young woman who at first she thought was one of her students until she showed her identification.

"The Advocate?" Lee Ann frowned in confusion. The woman was a reporter for the Baton Rouge press. "All of the media for the college is handled by the main office." She started to open her door.

"Actually I'm here to speak to you."

"Me? About what?"

"I wanted to know your reaction to what transpired at the White House today."

Her guard went up. "I have no idea what you're talking about." She moved toward her car again.

"What's your take on Senator Graham meeting privately with the president about the education reform bill? Your father has run that committee for several years. We understand that you and Senator Graham have been seen quite a bit together. Did he tell you anything about the meeting?"

This time she did get her door open. If there was one thing she'd learned growing up in a political family is that when cornered by a reporter, claim ignorance. Never let them have the opportunity to quote you as saying anything. That was as much ingrained in each of the Lawson children as their ABCs.

"If you'll excuse me." She pulled open her car door and got behind the wheel, ignoring the woman's mouthed questions outside of her closed window.

Lee Ann backed out of her space and pulled out of the lot. Her hands were shaking. What was going on? She had no idea how much truth was in what she was told, but she was sure that there must be some kernel to have the press sniffing. And if it was true, why didn't Preston say something to her, warn her? Worse, if it were true, how would this affect her father?

She didn't have long to find out. The minute she walked in the door, Desiree greeted her. The fact that she was home so early from her job at the community board was enough of an alarm.

"I was in the office today and a reporter called about Preston."

Lee Ann briefly shut her eyes. She dropped her purse on the table in the foyer. "One stopped me in the parking lot."

"What's going on? Have you spoken to Preston?"

"No, I haven't. We're supposed to talk tonight. He said he had something to talk to me about. But he wouldn't go into detail about what it was."

"Daddy must be livid," Desiree groaned.

Lee Ann didn't want to think about it. Branford's outbursts were few and far between but legendary. And once you were the focus of his displeasure, you ultimately became persona non grata. In politics, you may as well walk away from your career. *Please don't let that be what happened with Preston,* she silently prayed. *Please.*

"I'm sure it's some ridiculous rumor that the press got wind of," Dominique said while the three sisters sat around the kitchen table, jumping every time the phone rang. Dominique had closed the office early and come straight home when she got the call from Desiree.

"How *are* things between you and Preston?" Dominique asked.

"Fine." She folded her hands. "At least I *thought* they were fine. I just wish I could talk to him before Dad calls. At least I would have some idea of what I'm working with."

"Have you tried Preston's cell?"

She nodded. "Voice mail."

"He'll call," Desiree said.

They were silent for a moment.

"Oh! I have some great news," Dominique said.

"What?"

"The grant that you helped me with. It went through. We're going to get the money to offer GED classes. I am so excited."

"Dom! Congratulations," Desiree said.

"That is wonderful."

"I couldn't have done it without you," she said sincerely. "That whole part of the organization is not my strength. I love dealing with the clients or going out and pitching the organization. If it were left up to me for funding, we would have been shut down a long time ago," she said, laughing lightly.

"It was your concept. Your step-by-step plan. You had all the information. All I did was put it together on paper."

"I really wish you would think about coming on board as a consultant."

Lee Ann shook her head. "I already have enough on

my plate. Between teaching and overseeing Daddy's local office and his agenda, I have plenty to do."

"And managing your love life," Dominique teased, nudging Lee Ann's arm.

Lee Ann's face heated. Even though her sisters were grown women, who she knew were not virgins, she'd never really discussed her personal life with them. They'd come to her over the years with their "boyfriend" problems. But since they'd become women, that part of their lives was only alluded to. And truth be told, as close as she was to them, she often felt like an outsider. She was the problem solver. The advice giver. The money loaner. She could never be part of the two. Not really. She wanted to change that. She jumped at the ringing of her cell phone. It was Preston's number.

She drew in a breath. "It's him. Excuse me for a minute." She walked out of the kitchen. "Hello?"

"Lee, its been pretty crazy around here today."

"Around here, too. What is going on? The reporters are saying that you met secretly with the president, possibly to undermine the education reform bill?"

"I did meet with him, but that's not the way it was."

"Not the way it was?" Her voice hitched a notch. "Then what way was it, Preston?" She paced as she waited.

"It's complicated."

Lee Ann halted mid-step. "Is that all you have to say? It's complicated! You're damn right it's complicated, Preston! I have reporters wanting to know my feelings about you going against my father on a bill that he's worked on for several years. And did I know you were cutting your own deal with the president—using your past relationship with him—" Hot tears of fury stung her eyes. "Of course I didn't know! I was blindsided like everyone else."

"There wasn't enough time—"

"You had enough time to set up the meeting, Preston, without saying anything. Not even to me. You didn't just wake up at your desk and say, 'You know what, I think I'll use my old friendship with the president to further my own agenda and screw over the man who helped me.'" Her voice shook and then a chill settled over her. "That's what it's been about from the beginning, hasn't it? It's what you're about... You use people to get what you want." Saying the words weakened her knees. She reached for the chair.

"Don't do this, Lee Ann."

She didn't hear his warning. "My father...me." Images of the two of them entwined together flashed in her head. "Was I a stepping stone, too, another honorable mention on your résumé!"

Her saber-sharp words stabbed so deep, sliced so many vital organs that to survive, for them to survive, he had to get away. "If that's what you think, Lee Ann, then there's nothing more for me to say."

Her breath stopped short. Was this it? Her thoughts veered in a dozen directions at once. Did she really believe the things she'd said? Was she right? Wrong?

Her lips tightened over the words but couldn't hold them back. "You're right. There is nothing else to say." She squeezed the phone in her hand, praying that he would say something to stop this speeding train. Tell her that she was crazy. That he would never do anything like that.

"Gotta go."

Those two damning words and the soft click of the call coming to an end exploded in her ear.

That night was the first night since they'd been together that they had not spoken before going to sleep, spending at least an hour talking about their day, laughing, whispering, promising…

Lee Ann curled on her side, one tear following after the other.

Chapter 14

It was early evening before Lee Ann actually got out of bed. She'd been hiding out in her room all day. She wasn't up to questions or conversation. She'd spent most of the day dozing off and on, reliving that awful conversation with Preston and wishing that she could take back the things that she'd said. Throughout the day she kept checking her phone, thinking that maybe she'd somehow missed a call or a text from him.

She pressed her head into the thick softness of the down pillows and threw her arm across her face. She should have heard him out—listened to what he had to say. Maybe it wasn't as incredibly horrible as it seemed. She moaned.

The sound of her sisters' voices and splashing water tugged Lee Ann out of bed. She went to her window. Desiree and Dominique were at the pool engaged in one of their favorite pastimes—swimming. A reluctant half smile graced her mouth. She went and took a long shower.

She looked in the closet one more time. Since Dominique had taken her shopping and pretty much become her fashion guru, the interior of her closet had taken on a whole new look. Gone were the dark corporate midcalf suits, replaced with fitted jackets, skirts that skimmed her knees, sleeveless tops in bold colors and silky fabrics, plenty of shorts to show off her legs, an assortment of jewelry and enough lingerie to open her own boutique. She finally decided on an outfit and went down to sit with her sisters.

"Put on a suit and get in," Dominique called out.

"I'll pass, thanks." She walked over to one of the lounge chairs and stretched out, thankful that she'd finally decided on a pair of navy-and-white-striped shorts and a sleeveless T-shirt.

"I'm surprised we haven't heard from Daddy, yet," Desiree said, pulling herself up on the deck. Dominique pulled up behind her.

"Yes, I was thinking the same thing. Maybe it was all about nothing," Lee Ann said, needing her hopes to be shared.

"I'm just saying it can't be too serious if Daddy hasn't called trying to blow the roof off the house," Dominique added, wrapping a towel around her waist.

The sisters all turned at the sound of the sliding door opening.

"Daddy," they chorused in astonishment.

"You girls put some clothes on. I brought company home."

They shared a look.

"Who?" Dominique asked.

"The boy who's been stirring up all the ruckus up on the Hill."

"Preston is here—with you?" Lee Ann squeaked in disbelief.

"Up front," he said, with a toss of his head toward the house.

Lee Ann pushed up from the chair, hurried over to her father and kissed his cheek. "I'm so sorry. I didn't know—"

"Why don't you go on up front and let your young man explain."

Her throat tightened. She pressed her lips together to keep them from trembling and went in search of her "young man."

Preston was pacing the living room floor so intent that he didn't hear Lee Ann enter the room.

"Preston…"

Her voice caught him midstride. "Lee." He crossed the space before she could take her next breath, and then she was in his arms, his lips covering hers.

"I'm sorry," he whispered in her hair.

"I'm sorry, too. I should have listened…"

She stroked his hair, his face, the curve of his back as if assuring herself that he was really there and not part of the dream that she had of him every night.

"We need to talk."

"I know." She eased back and looked at him, hoping to see some hint of what brought him there.

"Come, I only want to tell this once, and it's really all thanks to your father."

* * *

Preston sat opposite Branford in the study with the sisters sitting around them. Preston was leaning forward, resting his arms on his thighs as he spoke, looking at each person in turn.

"I always believed from the time I set foot in the Senate that I wanted to be involved in education reform. I believe it is at the root of so many of our nation's problems. Lack of a good education creates the downhill snowball effect. No education, lack of employability, no jobs leads to no income, so they get welfare or rob and steal. And we wind up paying to take care of them in jails or in shelters." He straightened up. "But the educational system we have is broken. It doesn't work, and it doesn't serve our children."

"So Preston here had some different ideas about how to provide education," Branford said, picking up the explanation. "Community-based schools, run by the parents and the teachers…" He went on to explain his idea.

"It sounds incredible," Lee Ann said. "And do-able."

"In an ideal world," her father interrupted, "Preston knew it would never get out of committee without some real muscle behind it, and I have to admit that when he brought the idea to me I had my doubts. But he said that he wanted me to know what he was doing, that he didn't want me to think he was trying to step over me to get to the president, and I gave him my blessing."

Lee Ann looked at Preston and felt like bursting with pride.

"It definitely helped that we'd worked together in the past, but without your father's full support…"

"So—" Branford blew out a long breath and slowly stood "—the press only got it half right as usual." He chuckled on his way out of the room. "I'm going to bed."

"Night, Daddy."

"Good night, sir."

"Well, I guess we should leave you two alone," Desiree said, nudging Dominique, who had made herself very comfortable on the couch. "Dom!"

"What?"

Desi kept jerking her head toward the door.

Dominique pulled herself up. "You're going to get a crick in your neck if you keep that up," she said on her way out.

"What a day," Preston said, stretching his arms over his head.

"I can't tell you how proud I am—not only about your brilliant plan but how you handled it. And how sorry I am about everything that happened between us." Her eyes moved slowly across his face. "I know my father is not an easy man. He's stubborn and opinionated, pigheaded, handsome, brilliant, charming and driven." Her voice softened. "Just like you."

"Your father didn't get to where he is by making enemies and stepping on people's necks. He did it by being honest, no matter what the cost and sticking by his beliefs. It's the kind of career I want to have."

She reached across the space and took his hand. "I love you."

"Love you right back." He kissed the back of her hand.

"You must be exhausted."

"I am," he said while stifling a yawn. "Come home with me."

She smiled seductively. "You need your rest."

"I need you more."

"Are you sure?"

"Positive. And I can guarantee that I will be totally revitalized once I get you over there."

The moment they crossed the threshold of his house, Preston took Lee Ann into his arms. He caressed her cheek with his fingertips, trailing down the curve of her neck, setting shivers of delight that shimmied through her body.

She sighed with pleasure, and the sweet sound of it dipped down to Preston's soul. Her mouth was just as sweet and giving as much as she was receiving.

Lee Ann wrapped her arms around his neck—the desire to give herself totally to him pounding in her veins.

"Let's go upstairs," he breathed in her ear.

"Lead the way."

He kissed the tip of her nose and then her eyelids as they walked up the stairs together. He opened his bedroom door, swept her up into his arms and crossed the room to his bed and eased them both down.

"I dream about you every night," she said softly.

"Now we can make it real," he said before taking her lips to his own in a long, deep kiss. Finally, he eased back then kissed her again, softly, almost tentative this time, teasing her.

Lee Ann felt it in every inch of her being. Her body hummed as pleasure rippled through her in gentle, steady waves. Every tense muscle loosened. Her thighs eased apart, and Preston's sure hands traced her lines and curves.

He took her hand and placed it on his hardened shaft. "I've been dreaming of you, too." He groaned and squeezed his eyes shut when she tightened her hand around him.

She unzipped his pants, and he pushed them down and kicked them aside. Slowly she took him back and stroked him, feeling the veins and muscles tense and ripple beneath her fingertips.

Preston gritted his teeth to keep from hollering, grabbed her hand, squeezed it once, then pulled her hand away from its hold. He eased her back onto the bed, unzipped her shorts and tugged them down over her hips, tossing them to the floor. She lifted up and pulled her shirt over her head.

Preston inched up on the bed and switched on the bedside lamp, casting a soft shadow across her body. "Let me see every inch of you tonight." He inched her panties over her hips, down her thighs and across her legs letting his fingers caress her all along the way, across her stomach, her inner thighs and ever so lightly across the tapered triangle that shielded the epicenter of her need.

Lee Ann writhed and gripped the sheet when Preston's thumb brushed back and forth across her clit. He caressed and massaged it until it stood firm and fully exposed from its protective sheath. Her body shuddered, and she cried out in blinding delight as his mouth and tongue replaced his fingers. Her head spun, and wave after wave of pleasure shot through her. The pleasure became so intense that it was almost unbearable.

Preston gripped her hips and quenched his thirst for her.

Lee Ann became a conduit for pleasure. Every nerve ending vibrated as his tongue flicked, laved and teased, and then he inserted one finger then another.

Her body stiffened and arched in response. He spread his fingers and gently slid them in and out. Her ebbing and flowing moans excited him, and when her thighs spread wider and her body opened completely, he knew that he had her on the edge of coming.

"Ohhhh, ohhhh…yesss."

He reached around her and into his drawer and pulled out a condom even as he continued to bring her toward ecstasy.

"You do it," he said in a ragged whisper. He pressed his thumb against her clit, and her hips rose and bucked against his hand. "Now." He knew it was only sheer willpower that kept him from climaxing.

Lee Ann rolled the condom over the swollen head and down the bulging shaft.

Preston could barely contain himself. He moved between her parted thighs, keeping his fingers in place. He unsnapped her front closure bra, and her warm, full breasts welcomed him. Her nipples were hard and full, calling for his attention. He lowered his head and drew one into his eager mouth, and he pushed deep and hard inside her in one swift move.

A gush of air burst from her lungs as her insides instinctively gripped him, the muscles opening and closing around him.

"Ah, baby...I missed, missed you," he groaned, moving in long, slow strokes, willing himself to extend the incredible feeling that rocked them both. He pushed her legs back as far as her body would allow and sunk into the depths of her being, found her spot. She cried out once, twice, three times and then heaven and earth collided.

Lee Ann's entire body experienced wave after wave of unimaginable explosions, as Preston rode the tide to his own fantasy, until it burst in one powerful stream of release that erupted within her.

"How long can you stay?" Lee Ann whispered against his chest.

"I have to go back tomorrow."

Her heart sank. She knew that when she got involved with Preston that it would take work, that distance would be a factor. But it was becoming more and more difficult to leave him and watch him leave her. She pressed her head closer to his chest. How much longer could this go on and still work?

Chapter 15

The days turned into weeks and weeks into months, and Lee Ann and Preston tried to see each other as often as they could. But with the holidays approaching and the U.S. government preparing to shut down for winter recess, they were both busier than usual—he in Washington and Lee Ann back home overseeing her father's local office, juggling her classes and running the house. But they were desperately looking forward to spending the holidays together, and the Lawson holiday gathering was not to be missed.

Lee Ann, as usual, was in charge of all of the preparations, and she spent the bulk of her day on the phone with the caterers, the decorators and car services. It was exhausting but exciting, and as the big day drew closer and presents began to pile under the 18-foot spruce tree and the house was transformed into a picture postcard, Lee Ann was filled with a new kind of joy.

This would be the first time in years that she'd spent the special holiday season with the man she loved. She couldn't put into words how significant that was for her. She'd come a long way since she'd met Preston. He'd helped her to realize that she had the ability to be so much more than she'd allowed herself to be.

Little by little she'd loosened the reigns on her siblings, letting them get out of their own messes and figure things out for themselves. And the world didn't come to an end. She felt better and stronger. And oddly enough letting her sisters go had seemed to make them closer. They did things together, spent time at home together and Lee Ann had slowly begun to stop feeling like a third wheel.

As she looked around the house, taking in the twinkling lights, the enormous tree decorated in a multitude of red and white, the stack of presents, the banisters draped in garland and the side tables already laden with food for their incoming guests, she knew that she had much to be thankful for.

By seven, the house was filled from front to back. The five-piece band played in the background while tuxedoed waiters made sure that the wants of every guest was met.

Lee Ann was in her glory playing hostess, greeting guests, remembering everyone's name and something personal about them—a trick her mother taught her years ago—kissing cheeks and nodding in all the right places.

Her father was holding court, as usual, in the back room; the twins were the effortless social butterflies; Rafe was tucked away in a corner with his latest lady friend; and even Justin brought a date, a young lady from college.

Everyone was present and accounted for except for Preston, and as the first hour of the evening moved into the second, Lee Ann grew more anxious.

"Where's Preston?" Rafe asked, sliding up behind her. "Haven't seen him tonight."

Her stomach fluttered. "I don't know. He should have been here by now."

Rafe sipped his drink. "Hmm, probably stuck in traffic."

"I guess," she said absently, trying to look busy doing nothing besides secretly worrying. "Who are you with tonight? She doesn't look familiar, not that any of your dates usually do."

"Aw, sis, don't be mean. Her name is Angela."

"And how long will she be around?"

"As long as she likes."

Lee Ann arched a brow. "Really?"

"Of course." He kissed the top of her forehead. "They all are. Come on over, and I'll introduce you."

She dutifully followed him across the room while taking surreptitious glances in between moving bodies, hoping that Preston would appear. And just when she thought she would burst with worry she saw him coming out of the back room, side by side with her father. A wave of relief rushed through her. The jumpy feeling began to settle in her stomach. But when had he arrived, and why hadn't he let her know that he was there?

He glanced up and spotted her across the room. His entire expression lit up. and whatever frustrations she may have had began to vanish as he came toward her.

Preston walked right up on her so that their bodies brushed. She felt the blood pounding in her ears and the racing of her heart, and she wondered for the countless time if she would always feel this joy whenever she saw him.

"Hey." He took her hand.

"Hi. I was getting worried."

"You look beautiful."

"Thank you. What happened? Is everything okay?"

He looked at her as if taking her in for the very first time. His gaze was filled with wonder.

"Everything is wonderful." He slid an arm around her waist. "Dance with me." He didn't give her a chance to respond but swept her expertly onto the dance floor.

She couldn't stop looking at him. The sweet brown of his smooth skin, the dark, piercing eyes, embraced by slick sweeping brows. His mouth was suddenly new, full and lush, with a tiny dip at the top. Was that always there? she thought in wonder.

Lee Ann was sure she knew every inch of his body, but tonight, for reasons that she couldn't explain, she felt the urge to explore it: the arch of his broad back, the taut muscles of his chest, the ripples of his stomach, the hard thighs and the heft of his sex that had brought her unimaginable pleasure. The need grew so great that she moaned.

Preston held her closer, stroked her back. "You feel it too, don't you?"

She tilted her head back and looked up at him. "Yes."

"Let's find someplace quiet."

She took his hand, and they walked through the

crowd, bypassing the side rooms where overflow guests ate and talked. They walked through the kitchen, out into the yard to the edge of the property to the swing that was almost hidden by the weeping willow.

"Wow, I would have never found it."

"My secret hideaway."

He held the swing while she got on, and then he followed suit. He put his arm around her and pulled her close.

"You sure know how to throw a party."

She laughed lightly. "I was taught by the best," she said, a note of wistfulness in her voice.

"She would be very proud."

Preston drew in a long breath and let it go. "I've been thinking about this long-distance thing. It's really taken a toll on us this past year."

Fear began to build, tightening her throat.

"I don't know if I can do it for another year."

She couldn't breathe. This couldn't be happening.

"But I thought that if we at least had one roof that we could call our own…"

Her eyes flew to his face.

"…the property of Mr. and Mrs. Preston Graham that we'd find a way to make it work."

What was he saying? She couldn't get the words to make sense in her head.

"Marry me, Lee Ann. Share my life and my dreams, and let me share yours."

He reached into the breast pocket of his tux jacket and took out a perfect, sparkling diamond set on white gold. He held it in front of her. "Early Christmas gift. Say yes."

Her eyes stung and tears of elation fell over her lashes. "I love you so much."

"Is that a yes?"

She bobbed her head. "Yes."

Preston slid the ring on her finger. "We're going to make it work."

"I know."

He pulled her into his arms and sealed their commitment with a kiss.

"And if you're wondering," he said, still holding her, "I'm an old-fashioned guy. I spoke with your father. I wanted his approval. That's what I was doing in the back room."

"And what if he would have said no way?"

"You should know me well enough by now to know that I don't take no for an answer."

Lee Ann bubbled with happiness and pulled him into her arms.

Lee Ann couldn't remember how the rest of the night went. She was floating on a cloud. Finally the last guest waved their goodbyes and the caterers had taken away their carts and trays and the family settled down in front of the tree, sighing in contentment that it was finally over. Another success under their belt.

"Congrats, sis. You did it again," Rafe said, saluting her with his half-filled glass.

"Thanks." She moved closer to Preston.

Branford cleared his throat. "Is that all you have to say, Lee? Sure there's nothing you want to tell us?"

All eyes turned in her direction, and when she looked

at Preston he had a smirk on his face. She glanced from her father back to Preston. She'd been set up!

She stood up dramatically. "Well, if you must know…" She flung her hand out in front of her.

Her sisters leaped up and squealed, jumping up and down and taking turns looking at her ring and holding it up to the light.

Justin came over. "Congrats, sis, I'm happy for you." He kissed her cheek and shook Preston's hand.

Rafe walked over and spun her around in a hug. "Told ya, follow my advice," he whispered in her ear. Lee Ann swatted his arm. He set her on her feet and looked down into her eyes that reminded him of his mother. "I'm happy for you. I really am." He turned to Preston and stuck out his hand. "Welcome to the family. Now that we have two senators, it takes the pressure off me." He winked at Preston. "You do right by my sister."

"You don't have to worry about that."

Rafe clapped him on the back. He turned to the room, a bit wobbly on his feet. "I am heading home. I will see you all tomorrow."

Branford pushed up from his chair. "You're not getting behind the wheel tonight. Go on up to your room and sleep it off."

Rafe swayed. "Don't you ever get tired of telling people what to do? You run your house like you run the country—with no excuses. Everything has to be by the letter."

"You're drunk," Branford said in dismissal.

"You were so busy being in charge that you couldn't let go long enough to take care of Mama."

"Rafe!" Lee Ann shouted.

"You wanted to make me into you. I'll never be you. I don't want to be you." He laughed and stumbled, catching his fall by grabbing the side of the mantel.

"Come on, man," Justin said, taking his arm.

Rafe shrugged him off. "Now you have your very own boy wonder to mold into your likeness." He tossed his head back and laughed and laughed until he started to cry.

Dominique and Desiree were frozen. They'd never seen Rafe like that before. It was as if their invincible brother was suddenly broken and they couldn't bear to watch.

"Rafe..." Lee Ann said gently, putting her arms around him. "Let me walk you upstairs."

His shoulders shook, and Lee Ann could feel his hurt in her own heart. She let him lean on her, and she half walked, half dragged him upstairs and got him to his old room.

As soon as he got to the bed he turned on his side. Moments later he drifted to sleep. Lee Ann backed out of the room and closed the door behind her.

When she returned downstairs, her father was gone.

"He's in his study," Desiree said.

Lee Ann squeezed Preston's hand. "I'll be back. I need to talk to him."

"Sure. Take your time."

Lee Ann tapped lightly on the partially opened door before stepping in. Her father was sitting in the dark. His back was to the door so that he faced the window that looked out onto the yard.

"Daddy..."

"Lovely party."

She stepped closer and stood behind his chair.

"You did a real good job. You always do. Just like your mother. Don't know what I'd do without you."

She came around and knelt by his side. She covered his hand that gripped the armrest of the chair.

"Those girls will be all right. Desi has a good head and Dom…well she's coming along." He drew in a ragged breath. "I'm proud of her. Justin is turning into a fine young man. I have you to thank for that. Half his life his mother was sick and then she was gone."

"Daddy, why are you talking like this? You're scaring me."

"When a son turns against his father in his own house…" He sighed so heavily his body vibrated. "It's true what he said."

"No, it's not. Rafe was drinking too much. You can't pay that any attention."

"That's just it!" He slammed his hand down. "I wasn't paying attention. I let my family, my wife pass me by while I was riding off on my ideals. I want so much for Raford. He has it in him to be great. But he's trying so hard not to be me that he'll never see it."

He finally turned to her, and she could see in the moonlight that he'd been crying.

"Preston has the potential to be great. He has everything it takes to lead a country. Not everybody has it, but he does. You be there to help him choose wisely. Don't let him sacrifice family for a career. Because when the career comes to an end—and one day it will—you have nothing to come home to." He squeezed her chin. "Promise me that you'll remember that."

She nodded, unable to get the words out.

"Go on now. Me and Rafe will make it up. We always do. Go ahead. I'll be fine. I'm just going to sit here for a minute."

Lee Ann slowly stood, then leaned down and kissed his forehead. "I'll see you in the morning."

By the time she came back to the front room, only Preston remained. He got up as she approached.

"How is he?"

"Talking crazy. It was a little scary."

"What do you mean?"

"I don't know. It was like he was going down the list of attributes of each of us kids. He kept talking about how he shortchanged us by pretty much checking out of the family for the benefit of his career."

She sat down, and Preston sat beside her. He took her hands and enfolded them in his.

Lee Ann looked at him. "He said that you have what it takes to go all the way, to run a country. But he said that I need to be there to help you make the right choices and never to choose your career over your family." She rested her head against Preston. "That's his biggest regret. That and what he feels he's done to Rafe—never really giving him a fair deal." She sighed and felt like crying on what should have been one of the happiest days of her life.

"Maybe you should stay here tonight."

She turned her head to look at him. "I want to be with you tonight. I need to be with you tonight."

"Are you sure?"

She nodded her head.

"Okay, let's go."

Lee Ann went up to her room and tossed a few things in a bag, peeked in on Rafe and let her sisters know that she was leaving.

Preston opened the door to his house, and Rocky came trotting up to greet them.

"Hey, boy. Look, I brought company."

Lee Ann scratched his head. "Hey, Rocky. I'm going to be your new mommy. Look." She shoved her ring toward him. He sniffed and walked away. Lee Ann broke out laughing. "He could pretend to be interested."

"Well, I'm plenty interested." He grabbed her in his arms and kissed her like he'd been longing to do for hours. "Hmm," he sighed, running his hands along her sides.

"Did you bring me over here to seduce me?" she asked against his lips.

"Come with me. Let me share with you the real art of seduction."

"Where are we going?"

He took her hand and led her upstairs to the bathroom. He turned on the shower. Within moments, the room began to fill with steam.

She angled a look at him. "And what do you have on your mind?"

He came to stand in front of her. "I need you to put all of your inhibitions to the side. Whatever you were holding back, I want you to let go. And believe in me."

Lee Ann's pulse kicked up a notch as Preston's eyes locked with hers, and he unzipped her dress from the back and one by one pulled the straps over her shoulders.

The rise of her breast came into view, and he grazed his fingers ever so lightly across them. Lee Ann shivered all the way to her toes. He pushed the dress down, and she shimmied it down her hips until she was standing before him in only an itty bitty black thong.

A deep groan rumbled in his chest as he hooked his fingers around the band of her thong and helped her step out of it.

Preston got undressed, never letting his gaze drift from Lee Ann. He pushed his discarded clothes to the side and then took her hand as they stepped into the shower.

"Give me your back," he said.

She turned so that her back was facing him. He reached for the shower gel that he kept in the shower caddie and began to lather her back, her behind, her inner thighs and her calves then with smooth, circular strokes. He moved ever so slowly along the curves of her body until every inch of her was covered.

Lee Ann braced her hands against the wall as the erotic caress intensified. She whimpered when the pads of his fingers teased the undersides of her breasts.

"Look at me."

Slowly Lee Ann turned around. Preston was intent and focused on her. His eyes felt like they burned across her skin.

She wanted him there and then. No preamble. No more teasing.

Preston devoted the same attention to her front, caressing, massaging, stroking. Then he rinsed her off before he switched places, quickly soaped, rinsed and got out.

He picked her up dripping wet and took her to his bed. He stood above her, looking over every inch of her as if seeing her for the very first time.

"Preston..."

He shook his head no.

Her gaze rolled up and down his body, and she drew in a shaky breath. She was always awed to see him fully aroused and knew what he could do when he was.

Preston sat down on the side of the bed and took the pillows and propped them beneath her head. Then he took another pillow and placed it beneath her hips.

He ran a finger down the center of her body, and it felt like an electric current was running through her. He knelt between her slightly parted thighs. He pushed them a little more apart and lifted her knees so that the epicenter of her essence was open to him.

He began to massage her breasts in slow, circular motions, cupping them, lifting them, using his palms to rotate around her nipples.

Lee Ann's breath stuttered in her chest as pleasure rolled through her.

"In and out," he coaxed. "Take a breath." He began working his way down her body in the same slow motions, covering her with the electric heat of his hands, charging her flesh wherever he touched.

Her thighs were trembling when he touched her between her legs. He pressed his palm firmly against it, cupped it, held it like a treasure then moved his hand tightly up and down. He gently squeezed her outer lips between his thumb and forefinger, and when he was sure that she was ready, he told her to inhale and hold it and he held her pulsing bud between his fingertips.

"Ahhhh!" Her hips rose. Her legs trembled from her hips to her ankles.

"That's it, baby. Let the feeling take you." With his palm facing upward, he gently inserted his middle finger, moving it in and out, taunting and teasing the spongy wall. Her entire body vibrated. A moan so deep pushed up from her soul and enveloped her.

Wave after wave of pleasure pushed through her as Preston continued his most intimate massage of her.

For what seemed like hours, Preston adored her body, bringing her to heights that had her screaming for release, shuddering under the onslaught of pleasure that was so divine that she felt herself shatter into millions of satisfied pieces.

He placed tender-loving kisses all over her body before covering her with a sheet as she slipped into a deep, satisfied sleep.

Chapter 16

When the phone rang it seemed like they'd barely gone to sleep.

Lee Ann mumbled and buried her head deeper beneath the sheet. Preston turned on his side to tune out the offending noise.

The phone kept ringing.

Lee Ann poked her head above the covers and squinted against the morning light. The ringing stopped. Just as she was settling back down, the phone started ringing again.

"Press…the phone."

"Let the machine get it."

She flopped back down on the pillow, and the ringing started again.

"Oh! Either you answer it or I will."

"Answer it then," he said from underneath his pillow.

Lee Ann reached over him to get the phone and dragged it across his back. "Good morning, Senator Graham's residence. Desi?" She bolted upright. "What? When. Okay, okay. I'll be there. I'm on my way."

She jumped out of bed.

"What is it?" Preston sat up and rubbed his eyes. "What's going on?"

"It's Rafe. He went out in the middle of the night on his bike. He ran into one of the dividers and was thrown. They're trying to stabilize him in the emergency room." She began to shake.

Preston threw the covers off. "I'm coming with you. You're not driving alone." He grabbed his clothes, and they moved side by side in the bathroom to get ready.

"Buckle up," Preston instructed as he put the Lexus SUV into gear.

Lee Ann had barely said a word since she got the call from Desi. Her thoughts were spinning in a million different directions at once.

"I should have stayed."

"What?" He stole a quick glance at her as he sped across the intersection.

"I should have stayed. If I'd been there I could have stopped him." She pressed her fist to her mouth.

"Lee, don't do that to yourself. It's not your fault. There's no guarantee that if you had been there, you would have heard him or been able to stop him. You can't be responsible for what someone else decides to do."

"But I knew he was hurting—hurting in a way that I've never seen before. Rafe is always the image of cool,

in control. I've never even seen him drink like that."
She shook her head, still in denial.

"Believe it or not, Lee, there will always be things about your family that you won't know. Rafe must have some things bugging him that he hasn't let anyone know about, not even you."

She drew on a shuddering breath. "He has to be all right, Preston."

He reached across the gears and squeezed her hand. "He's going to be okay, baby."

Her bottom lip trembled. "Welcome to the family."

"I'm looking forward to it." He took the next left and took the expressway across town.

Lee Ann and Preston pushed through the revolving door of Brook Memorial Hospital, checked signs as they walked, looking for the information desk.

Lee Ann rushed forward to the nurse's station. "Excuse me, Raford Lawson, Senator Lawson's son, my brother. He was in a motorcycle accident." Her heart was thundering.

Preston kept her from leaping over the desk in her frenzy to get to her brother, with a firm hold around her waist.

The nurse looked at her computer screen, checked the most recent information and stood. "He's still being accessed in emergency. Right down the hall through the double doors. Stop at the intake desk."

"Thank you."

Preston took her hand and kept her from running. "Wait one second."

She stopped.

He braced her shoulders and leaned down so that he could look directly into her eyes. "You need to pull yourself together. Take a breath. I'm here. Okay?"

She nodded, her eyes glistening. They headed down the corridor.

Preston pushed open the swinging doors. Everywhere they looked, doctors, nurses and orderlies were racing in and out of the curtained room. Machines beeped, metal equipment clanged. And tinsel and garland decorated the desks.

They hurried over to the intake desk.

"Can I help you?"

"My brother, Raford Lawson…"

The nurse checked the board behind her. "He was taken up for a CT scan. I believe the family is in the waiting area. Make a left at the end of the hallway."

"Thank you."

They walked past one curtained room after another even as EMS rushed by them with a stretcher carrying a middle-aged man on a backboard. They made the turn and found the glass-enclosed waiting room.

Desi, Dominique and Justin were huddled together. Their father sat alone on the other side of the small room, looking as if he'd aged ten years overnight.

All eyes turned in their direction when they came through the door.

Desi leaped up. "I'm so glad you're here." She practically fell into Lee Ann's arms.

Lee Ann looked down at Dominique. She kneeled down in front of her. "Dom…"

Dominique looked at her sister. Her eyes were red and puffy. The nerves twitched beneath the skin of her face. "I didn't hear him leave," she said, her voice wobbling.

"It's not your fault, Dominique. You couldn't have known," she said, repeating the assurances that Preston had given her. She focused her attention on her baby brother. "Are you okay?" He nodded.

Lee Ann stood and turned in the direction of her father. Preston took a seat with Lee Ann's siblings.

"Daddy." Lee Ann approached her father as you would a wounded animal. You knew they were hurt, but you didn't know if they would turn on you in their pain.

His shoulders began to shake, and the silence of his anguish was louder than any cries. Lee Ann sat next to him, offering soothing sounds and words of comfort as they waited for word from the CT scan.

"Senator Lawson?"

Branford glanced up. A nurse was in the doorway. She stepped in. "Your son had the CT scan. He's going to be admitted. The doctor will come to speak with you shortly."

"How is he? What did the test show?" Branford demanded.

"I'm sorry, but you'll have to wait to speak to the doctor." She turned and left the room before she could be bombarded with any more questions that she couldn't answer.

It was more than an hour before a doctor appeared. "Senator…"

"Yes."

"I'm Dr. Wilson from neurology. Your son is very lucky. He has a pretty bad concussion and a hairline fracture above his eye, sprained wrist and a bruised rib. It could have been a lot worse. We'll need to keep him for a few days, make sure he's stable. He's resting now and comfortable. He's going to have a whopper of a headache, and his left eye is going to be swollen for a while as the fracture heals."

"Can we see him?" Lee Ann asked.

"Not now. But maybe this evening. He's resting, and he needs to be constantly monitored so that he doesn't slip into a coma. Visitors would not be good now. The nurse can let him know that you were here. In the meantime, get some rest and come back this evening. If there is any change, you will be called immediately."

"Thank you, Doctor," Lee Ann said. She turned to the family. "There's nothing we can do now. He's resting. He's stable. We can see him tonight."

Preston kept a protective arm around her shoulder.

"Let's all go back to the house."

They filed out and returned to the Lawson mansion and were met by news vans parked outside their property.

They drove around back and parked and entered the house from the patio.

"How do those vultures find out about every blasted thing?" Branford fumed as he stormed into the house.

"They pick up information from police radio, hearing about accidents," Preston offered.

"I'm going to fix some coffee," Lee Ann said. "Is anyone hungry?"

Nods came from all around.

"Figures," she joked.

"I'll help. I'm pretty handy in the kitchen," Preston said, going to the sink to wash his hands.

She tiptoed and kissed him. "Thanks."

"It's going to be okay, you know."

She leaned against him for a moment. "I know."

Chapter 17

Rafe remained in the hospital for a week—until two days before Christmas. Lee Ann had served as the family spokesman and gave all the news outlets the same response. "No comment."

The doctor said that Rafe would experience periodic headaches, but they would eventually subside and go away entirely. They wanted him to come back after the holidays for a follow-up.

When he came home, looking a little worse for wear, he at least had sense enough to act humble. And as usual, his sisters doted on him hand and foot.

"I really screwed up this time," he admitted while he and Lee Ann sat on the patio.

"Yes, you did. You need to talk to Dad, Rafe. I mean really talk to him about what's on your heart, why you're so angry. He lost Mom, too."

Rafe looked away. "I know. I will."

"Promise me."

"Promise. Speaking of promises, have you two set a date?"

"No. Not yet. We have to work out our schedules."

Rafe nodded. "I'm happy for you. Preston is a great guy, but he's the lucky one."

She leaned over and kissed him. "Thanks, sweetie."

Christmas was quiet, just the family and the soon-to-be new addition, Preston. They exchanged gifts, swapped stories and it looked like Rafe and Branford were actually trying to talk to each other.

This was probably the first major holiday when Rafe wasn't rolling all around the city with a woman on his arm. Instead, he entertained them with a solo performance on his sax.

Lee Ann watched her father's reaction. She could tell that he was completely surprised and realized for the first time that Rafe was a born musician. His small, captive audience applauded loudly.

"Thank you, thank you. Well, if there are no tips, I'm going to head up to bed," Rafe said. "Have a good night."

"We're going to a party," Dominique announced on behalf of Desiree and Justin.

"Keep an eye on your sisters, son."

"I will. Night." He followed his sisters out.

Branford swirled the last of his brandy in his glass. "Have you settled on a date?"

"No. Not yet."

"I've been trying to get her to settle on a date," Preston said, giving her a hug.

"It would make me very happy if you took your vows on your mother and mine's wedding day."

"Valentine's Day?" Lee Ann said.

Branford nodded. A soft smile shadowed his mouth. "She told me if we get married on Valentine's Day you can never forget our anniversary." He chuckled lightly. "She was right, you know."

Preston turned to Lee Ann. "What do you think, Lee?"

"I…" She looked from one man to the other. She got up. "We don't have to make a decision right this minute." She walked out.

"Excuse me." Preston followed her out into the kitchen. "Lee, what is it?"

She kept her back to him. "Nothing."

He took her shoulders and turned her around. "Way back when we promised each other honesty."

She averted her gaze.

"So you want to tell me the real reason why you don't want to set a date?"

She needed to find the right words so that he would understand that her indecision had nothing to do with loving him but loving herself enough.

"They still need me. My father, Justin, Rafe. I still have nightmares about what happened to Rafe—if I had been there…"

"Stop right there. You have spent the better part of your life taking care of everyone else. You need them to need you to make you feel worthy. But Lee, you deserve so much more than that. I want to do that for you. I want to take care of you. I want you to enjoy life—with me. And that will never happen if you continue to believe that your family can't live without you. I don't want to live without you, but I will. And as much as you don't want to admit it they will all eventually move on with their lives, as well. And then where will you be?" He stared at her for a long moment. "I'm going home." He turned and walked out.

Lee Ann lay in bed thinking about what Preston had said. She knew it was true. She was scared—scared to step into a new life where she wasn't sure of her role of being taken care of instead of the other way around. She didn't know what that was like.

But ever since Preston had come into her life everything had been different and new and exciting. And he never let her be afraid of the person she was becoming. He was there to catch her, encourage her, love her.

She felt as though she was standing on a precipice, looking out into the future that she couldn't yet see, but deep in her heart, in her soul, she knew that Preston was there waiting for her.

But he wouldn't wait forever. She reached on her nightstand for the phone.

Preston answered on the second ring.

"I was thinking that if I want to make sure you never forget our wedding anniversary we should make a date to remember."

"And what did you come up with?"

"Valentine's Day."

"I think it would be a perfect day to remember our wedding day *and* your mom."

Tears of happiness sprung from her eyes. "I love you."

Epilogue

The wedding of Lee Ann Lawson and Preston Graham was the social event of the season. The guests were dotted with politicians, entertainers, lifelong friends and family.

Branford proudly gave his first daughter's hand to a man who he knew would do great things in the world and would make his daughter happy. His only wish was that their love would be as great as his and his beloved Louisa.

Rafe played the wedding march on his sax, and Lee Ann had never heard it sound sweeter. Her beautiful sisters and her handsome brother stood witness to their union, and Paul stood as Preston's best man.

And when Preston slipped the wedding band on her finger and she slid the band on his, Lee Ann knew that even though she was stepping out into a new, unchartered life, she wasn't leaving her family. They would never stop needing and loving each other. Now she would begin a family of her own, with the man who made her believe in herself and her worthiness, taught her what real love was. She would spend the rest of their lives letting him know what a great job he did.

"Ladies and gentlemen, I present to you Mr. and Mrs. Preston Graham!"

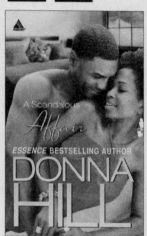

Fru·gal·is·ta [froo-*guh*-**lee**-stuh] *noun*
1. A person who lives within her means and saves money,
but still looks good, eats well and lives *fabulously*

THE TRUE STORY OF HOW
ONE TENACIOUS YOUNG WOMAN
GOT HERSELF OUT OF DEBT
WITHOUT GIVING UP HER
FABULOUS LIFESTYLE

NATALIE P. MCNEAL

Natalie McNeal opened her credit
card statement in January 2008
to find that she was a staggering
five figures—nearly $20,000!—in
debt. A young, single, professional
woman, Natalie loved her lifestyle
of regular mani/pedis, daily
takeout and nights on the town
with the girls, but she knew she
had to trim back to make ends
meet. The solution came in the
form of her *Miami Herald* blog,
"The Frugalista Files." Starting in
February 2008, Natalie chronicled
her journey as she discovered how
to maintain her fabulous, single-
girl lifestyle while digging herself
out of debt and even saving for
the future.

THE *Frugalista* FILES

Available wherever books are sold.

HARLEQUIN®

REQUEST YOUR FREE BOOKS!

2 FREE NOVELS
PLUS 2 *FREE GIFTS!*

KIMANI™
ROMANCE

Love's ultimate destination!

KROM11

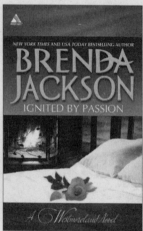
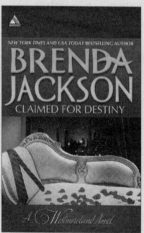

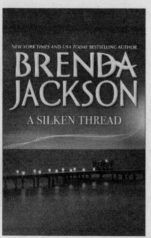